HIGH STAKES

LILLY CAIN

High Stakes

All I ever wanted is happening this weekend.

Or at least it might happen. If I don't screw it up. A lot can go wrong when you are sneaking around a Las Vegas hotel between a poker tournament and a romance writer's convention. And secretly attending both. More can go wrong when the one man you ever really wanted is there too, and he's watching. He's like a spy on a mission, always trying to keep me out of trouble.

He saved me once from drowning. He's my brother's best friend and I've wanted him since I was old enough to know what that means. But for him I've been off limits, the stakes were too high.

How could I resist making him the hero of my book? How will he react when he finds out?

Warning: This book contains awkward situations, fan-girling, laughter, heat, and love!

High Stakes by Lilly Cain

ISBN: 978-1-77521-203-4

Published by Lilly Cain

Cover design by Candice Gilmer
FlirtationDesigns.com

Discover other titles by Lilly Cain www.lillycain.com

Copyright © 2018 by Lilly Cain

For my writing friends - Sara, Renee, Cathy, and Donna.
And always, to my readers.

"WHAT DO YOU THINK, we go hit the tables after we get done here? Get some practice in?" Connor grinned at her. She couldn't help but grin back. Her big brother never seemed to run out of enthusiasm when it came to poker. They'd been standing in line for ten minutes, which wasn't bad, but there were at least a dozen people ahead, waiting to register at The Princess Resort, Las Vegas. She shifted her shoulder bag. The thing weighed a ton, but she wasn't about to put it down with Connor right beside her. Knowing him, he'd pick it up for her and then demand what made it so blasted heavy.

One manuscript, 347 double-spaced pages of love, lust and happy ending. *Her* manuscript. The thought made her want to do a little dance, right here in the lobby. *Jenn Riley, author.*

The line shuffled forward. Although there were three clerks on the hotel registration desk, getting checked in was taking forever. The place was huge, and the signs of the two ongoing events everywhere—the poker tournament she was playing in with her brother and his two friends and the romance writers' conference taking place in the larger ballrooms and meeting venues. The writers' conference she planned to secretly attend.

Connor and his friends had no idea she'd agreed to come with them when their fourth had broken a leg at his job, only because she could get to the writers' con from the poker tourney simply by crossing the hotel lobby. Her brother had teased her mercilessly about her love for romance novels when growing up, and if he heard she'd written one...

She shook her head.

Connor frowned. "What, you jetlagged?"

"Uh, a little. I think I might just chill a little, grab a swim and some time by the pool. Soak up some desert heat," she murmured distractedly.

Connor sighed but accepted her plan and then rambled on about the tournament, who he thought might be there this year, how tough they were. Like they hadn't gone over it at home. And at the airport. And on the plane. She stifled a sigh. The team competition worked on points, each player in their own division, and Connor had a hundred strategies, or more, since he had a female player on his team this time and could enter the new division. She liked poker, loved it, really. It was fun and she was good, thus the invite when Connor needed a fourth. But what she wouldn't give to go over and say hello to the authors gathering near the bar. They had to be authors. All women, gathered in circles, getting glasses of wine and talking about...what? Their new plot? Who had what book coming out next? She wet her lips and shuffled ahead in line.

Minutes later they were registered into adjoining rooms, Jenn in one and Connor in the other. His poker-partner buddies were apparently already checked into their rooms on the floor above. Connor texted them as Jenn watched a large screen to the right of the registration table. Conference information scrolled over the panel. She chewed her lip when she read the registration times for both events. *Damn.* Nearly the same time for both, and on opposite sides of the hotel. She'd have to catch the late registration for the writers' conference.

She walked with Connor to the elevator. The noise as they passed the bar was amazing, the place abuzz with what had to be a hundred women, all chatting and laughing, drinks in hand. She let a little wave of jealousy slide through her. If she'd had a little more money, she would have been here on her own instead of with her brother. She'd be in there with those women, meeting and greeting and rubbing shoulders with the authors she read every night. Soon though. After two years of playing with her book, it was done. Her career as a writer was about to begin and her life was about to change.

She dropped off her luggage in the room, nice enough for a hotel this size but she wouldn't have much time to enjoy it. Then it was off to explore and maybe meet up with the one author she did know at the convention, Nancy Clarke, a seasoned veteran of these events who helped with online pitch classes. It would be nice to finally put a face with the name.

She had more than one plan for the weekend, after all. Excitement zipped through her as she headed back down the elevator and detoured toward the pool. She had to at least say she'd seen it.

This trip was all about changing her life. Starting her writing career, placing high enough in the tournament to win the cash she needed to have the freedom to start her next novel without working.

She watched an older lady in an elegant pantsuit chatting with two younger women in suits near a large pool tent marked with the convention logo. Was that who she thought it was? Her heart beat a little harder. *Hello, fangirl moment.*

No way was she missing this opportunity.

She strode toward her—*the Nora*—and almost bumped into a young woman carrying drinks toward the tent. Jenn swerved, fought for balance, lost. At the last second, she threw her bag to the safety of a nearby lounger. It was the least she could do for her literary baby before she ended up in the deep end.

Unfortunately, she never had learned to swim.

A large, warm hand grabbed her by the shoulders and dragged her to the surface. She struggled, a bit desperate to get out of the water, but more so not to drown in front of her idol. Seconds later she was unceremoniously dumped on the tiles beside the pool where she sputtered for a moment before she noticed the hands running over her body and moved to protest. Only she couldn't quite catch her breath.

She looked up into a gorgeous set of big, blue eyes. Adrian D. Cooper. His serious, concerned expression heated her from cheeks to toes. As usual, he wore a baseball cap, and she fought the urge to flip it off and run her fingers through the dark brown curls underneath.

Dear Lord. Goal number three, alive and breathing. She'd wanted this man forever. Adrian had been her brother's best friend since they were all kids, and he never seemed to look at her as anything other than little Jenny, the girl he'd hauled choking out of the pool when she'd gone under at age eight.

Some days she wondered if she'd ever really come back

up. His blue eyes had sucked her in, and she'd caught herself drowning in them more than once. She'd fallen in love with him, and although he'd rescued her from the water, he'd never acknowledged the fact she needed more.

"I'm okay." But she stopped trying to brush his hands aside. Maybe it wasn't too late for CPR. A little mouth-to-mouth.

"You sure? Seems like we've been here before."

"Well, we have. Sure we couldn't have a little kiss like last time?" God. How did she let these things slip out of her mouth? But at least the flirtation had made him smile. So beautiful.

"I don't think you need resuscitation this time. You seem pretty conscious to me."

"Yeah." His gentle put-off hurt a bit, like it always did, but there was a touch of heat in his eyes beyond the amusement. Maybe there was hope.

There was a crowd gathering. Why did this sort of thing always happen to her? When she tried to sit up, he backed off enough to let her. "Just a little surprise dip."

"You don't swim." But he gave her a hand up. And when she shivered, he grabbed a towel from a shelving unit only a few steps away and wrapped her up, his hands gentle.

And if she leaned into him just a little... Was she so weak? Probably.

"Thanks." Jenn glanced around. Nora was gone—thankfully—but her bag was safe at the side of the pool on the lounger, and she snatched it up. Thank God for small things.

He threw the towel around her shoulders and tried to take the heavy shoulder bag from her.

"I've got this, thanks," she mumbled and hung onto her

bag. He, of all people, wasn't getting his hands on what was inside.

He tugged harder, pulling the weight from her for a moment—determined to be the gentleman, of course, a result of his Southern childhood and one of the things she'd always loved about him. She pulled back, and they wrestled for a moment over the heavy bag until Connor, who she hadn't noticed standing nearby, broke out in huge guffaw. She and Adrian had had a casual rivalry for years, another topic Connor loved to tease her about. She gave the bag one more tug and settled it on her shoulder, throwing Jenn off balance and nearly knocking into a lady passing by. All she needed was another trip into the pool. Adrian gave her a look and took her elbow, then led her back inside the hotel. She did her best to follow without stumbling.

If he read even a page of her book, he'd know exactly who it was about. And more, he'd see those nights when they'd laid in the grass watching stars as teens in a whole other way. She didn't want that, not exactly. She'd had years watching him and wanting him, but she wouldn't change that sweet time a bit. She just wanted...more...now.

The elevator was as packed as the rest of the hotel. She squeezed close to his six-foot-three frame until she could feel the heat coming off him. The soft scent of his cologne, woodsy and masculine, caught her. He looked fantastic yet casual in his jeans and button-down shirt. She, of course, now looked like a drowned rat.

Great. How was she going to reach goal number three when she still reminded him of that eight-year-old girl?

***

Damn, she looked good. This was going to be a very long

weekend. Her wet clothes clung to her like skin, showing every curve and even the tight points of her... God. He needed to keep his head down and zipper zipped and concentrate on the game. Jenn was not for him. Never mind that she'd somehow not only grown up over the last few years, but she was his type, perfectly. Five-foot-seven or so, and curvy. Straight, dark brown hair, brown eyes and full lips. Mmm, she had an ass he would like to take in his hands and—

"Ooof." The elbow to his side caught him by surprise.

"Wake up, bud." Connor laughed at him. "Long flight?"

"Ah, not bad." The flight in from Nevada had been a lot shorter than theirs from Texas. Jenn had a pretty blush running down her cheeks and neck, across her collarbone. Why again had he promised himself not to touch her?

"Thanks for saving Jenn *again*. How's your mom?" Connor'd had a fondness for Adrian's mother since they'd all grown up on the same street and his mother's cookies had saved the boys from near teenage starvation. Or at least imagined teenage starvation.

His mom. There was the reason he'd promised he'd keep his distance from Jenn. Right.

The elevator doors opened, and another couple somehow squished on, although they seemed to be headed down rather than up. Clearly they didn't give a crap about the tight quarters, but a bead of sweat slipped down the back of his neck as Jenn was forced to press against him, the curves of her ass thankfully resting against his hipbone rather than the rapidly hardening length of his cock. Thank God for the towel between them. All he needed was wet pants, and he'd be right back in high school.

Yup, lots of cold showers ahead.

A moment later, and they were standing in front of her

room. She opened her door and they trooped inside. Connor walked over to the adjoining room and opened it. The door to his side was already wide open and he strolled into his room.

"Adrian."

"Hmm...?" He'd taken a seat on her bed, where her shoulder bag was making a dent in the thick duvet. What was in that thing, rocks?

"I said, would you mind giving me some alone time? I need to change my clothes and crash for a while."

Adrian gave her a look. She didn't look tired. But he never knew with Jenn what she might be up to next. Then again, she might need rest. She'd never tried to get rid of him before. God, had she seen his hard-on? There was a time when she'd wanted him, they'd even shared a kiss before she went off to university, but he'd known better than to act on any impulses around her, and he'd thought she'd understood why. His stomach pitched into his shoes. Her girlish crush had meant more to him than he'd ever let on, maybe even to himself. That she'd wanted him even when he had been a jerk teenage boy had always made him feel better when things were crap in his life at home. But a crush was different than the lust-fest he had going on in his pants. Time to man-up. "All right, if you're sure you're okay. But registration starts pretty soon. And Connor wants to get a few warm up rounds in, size up the competition."

"I know. Not a problem."

Adrian walked through the door separating the siblings' rooms. Connor nodded at him. "Ready?"

"Jenn's not going. She's gonna rest for a bit."

"Seriously?" Connor looked incredulous, echoing Adrian's surprise. Connor shrugged. "Let's get going, check out the tables."

Adrian glanced back at Jenn. She'd grabbed her tote bag and was looking at something, not paying any attention to him. Her growing up was for the best. He shut the door and joined Connor in the hallway. They walked together to the elevator and caught a lift down to the lobby. Connor had been his friend for years, their tight bond formed when Adrian had moved with his mother to a house two doors down in the same small town in Texas. They'd needed a fresh start after his father had left them in Alabama with little more than the house mortgage, three months of unpaid bills, and a few hundred bucks in the checking account.

The friendship had lasted after Adrian moved to Nevada for work. Emails, calls and regular visits, plus the poker tourneys kept them from drifting apart like other childhood friends. That, and the fact that Adrian couldn't help but fall a little in love with their perfect family – mom, dad, sister, brother, and God only knew how many aunts, uncles and cousins. It was only his mom and his younger brother on his family tree. No need to add a father whose family was apparently made of assholes.

The elevator dinged, and they stepped out to the lobby, still crowded with people. The poker tournament took place on the left side of the hotel, in conference rooms managed by the casino half of the business. As they headed in that direction, Connor's steps grew faster. Adrian grinned. Cards had always been Connor's thing, while Adrian preferred sports and video games. Jenn had gone for books when she wasn't goading her brother and her brother's friends. The girl liked to tease. But to give Connor credit, he'd never shut his sister out and Adrian had enjoyed the time they'd all spent together. With only two years difference in age, Jenn had done her best to keep up with them in sports, and Connor had brought her along on movie nights and to local street parties. She'd fit in, and Adrian had found out she was pretty fun—for a girl.

They headed down the corridor to a second open area with a small bar and coat check. The small foyer split to the left into the main casino with its crashing noise and flashing lights of a few hundred slot machines, or over to the right, where the concert and banquet rooms lay. Since this was their third time at this hotel for the tournament, they knew the way and headed to the tournament rooms to take a look before registering.

As usual, a number of players had arrived early, and impromptu games were set up at several tables. Other, older players stood casually around and studied the hands and faces of those they would soon play against. There was serious money involved; the tournament held pots to be won at several levels. By registering as a group, the four wouldn't play against each other unless they made it into the final three games, but even if they didn't get that far, they could win more than enough in various, min tournaments that happened at the same time. The multiple ways to win made the trip worthwhile.

For Adrian, it wasn't about the money. He had enough, made plenty for his lifestyle and to send home to his mother. She'd never have to work three jobs supporting his brother as she had helping him through school with no help from their deadbeat dad. Now he had a role in a gaming company as a successful marketing advisor. So it wasn't about the kitty. Adrian came to be with Connor and the other guys. Seeing Jenn was a bonus, even if it was a bit of a strain. He wanted her, but indulging in an affair was out of the question.

What had happened to his mother would never happen to Jenn. She needed more than a few stolen days.

"Check out Brad, over there with the blonde."

Adrian scanned the room until he caught sight of their fourth group player. He sat at a table near the front of the room with two other players and a house dealer. He had his arm draped over a bored-looking blonde's shoulder while he gestured with his cards. Brad was another old friend, but he really hadn't managed to grow up much, from what Adrian could tell. He still chased every woman available.

Adrian laughed. "That's Zoe Stratton he's leaning all over. She's going to wipe his ass with his cards and send him home to mommy."

"The man has no clue. She's a professional player, wonder why she bothered to sit in?"

Adrian shrugged. They looked over the crowd, finding a few more players they knew and some of the heavy hitters they'd be lucky to sit with. It was great to be back, talking the game with Connor. Connor lived for the cards, but it was about the game more than the gamble. No betting problems for him. There were more women walking about than usual, probably drawn in by the special women's only tourney, an idea the casino supported heavily in an attempt to draw in video coverage from the major networks. More women meant more publicity. Jenn would fit right in and kick butt; she was more than a decent player and had beaten him a number of times.

"Shit. They're opening up registration early. Let me text Jenn." Connor pulled out his cell and tapped the screen.

"Sorry, sir, no phones in the tournament area." A security officer had walked over the minute Connor had pulled his cell from his pocket. He grimaced and put the phone away.

Adrian shrugged. "I'll go text her from the hall. She

could be asleep though. She said she needed to crash." He gave the guard a nod and walked out of the room. Players packed the hall and the small lobby, so he headed for the larger bar near the main lobby and entrance. Might as well kill two birds with one stone and get a couple of bottles of water while he was out.

He'd almost made it through the bar door when a flash of color caught his eye. A lady with a pink suit and a large brimmed hat with a long feather. A bit of overkill, there. But right beside her... He blinked and looked again. Yup, right beside her was the supposedly resting, too-tired-to-go-out Jenn.

CHAPTER TWO

SHE GAVE the men ten minutes to get going to the tables, taking the time to change into a simple yellow top and gray skirt and check her hair. Then she was out the door, dragging her heavy bag with her. You never knew, she could run into an editor or an agent in the elevator. That was why they called them elevator pitches after all, right? She was ready—she had business cards, printouts of her pitch and contact information, and if someone asked for her book, she could deliver it on the spot. She shivered as she imagined the feeling of trusting her work to a stranger. Her most intimate fantasies about Adrian. Not that anyone would know it was him. Or her.

The only real difficulty was that since registration for the writing conference hadn't opened, no one was wearing nametags and she wouldn't recognize any of the agents if they walked up and bit her. Editors either. Still, it didn't hurt to be prepared. A good motto, although it had always been Adrian that she imagined as a boy scout. She shivered again. Thoughts of Adrian as a boy scout made her think of his legs in shorts, which in turn made her think of the strong muscles he had in his thighs, and then her mind drifted upward...

The elevator was empty, but the ride down to the lobby gave her time to get a grip on herself. She'd tackle the issue of her and Adrian tonight, perhaps after they'd had a few drinks together after a casual game or two before the tourney opened. It could be a celebration all around. She patted her bag and the comforting weight of it. Time to make the changes she'd been dreaming about. A book deal, a card tourney, and Adrian. Not necessarily in that order, but hopefully before the weekend was over.

She hit the lobby and turned right toward the huge conference rooms. She should be perfectly safe to mingle with the writers while Adrian, Connor and Brad hung out with the poker teams on the opposite side of the hotel. She could juggle everything, it was simply an issue of time management.

Some of the ladies she'd seen earlier—one of them for sure had to have been Nora Roberts mixing with the little people—were gone now, maybe off to their rooms or attending to private meetings. But she headed for where the sign near the check-in had stated the registration table would be. Sure enough, there were volunteers setting out boxes of registration forms, checklists, and canvas bags stuffed with goodies and decorated with multiple author logos. One of the women wore a beautiful coral suit with a matching hat. It sported a long feather on one side. While the whole effect was a bit much, she had to admit the woman had confidence. After a moment of indecision, Jenn approached her. This was it, what she wanted. To get involved in the romance world. No point in being shy.

"Hi, uh, is this the registration table?" Great. The most obvious question, ever.

"Hello, dear. It is, but we aren't quite ready yet," the woman in the hat replied, her eyes barely resting on Jenn before flicking back over the volunteers and their progression. "But we might open a little early if you come back in fifteen minutes."

Perfect. She could be registered before the poker tournament registration opened.

"Jenn?"

Shit. She heard her name being called from across the room and looked over to catch a glimpse of Adrian's tall frame. What was he doing over here? She glanced around quickly and spotted a corridor a few paces away and made a dash for it. She hadn't said goodbye, but the organizer clearly had other things on her mind. And now, so did she. No way was she letting Adrian catch her over on this side of the hotel, not with her book in her arms. *His* book. Damn. She trotted down the hall and made a second quick turn, spied a ladies' room and dashed inside. The door swung shut behind her, and she sagged against the cool marble countertop of a dressing table.

She gave him five minutes. Maybe he hadn't seen where she went. Three steps out the door, and a hand caught her shoulder. She jerked around and came face to face with Adrian.

"There you are. They've opened registration early."

Registration? It took her a minute to realize he meant the poker tournament registration and not the romance writers' conference. Her heart barely had time to recover from the shock when it picked up speed again in reaction to his hand on her. He grazed his fingers along her arm and tried to lift the weight of her bag from her shoulder. When she shrugged away, his hand dropped, taking with it the sense of intimacy that perhaps she only imagined.

"C'mon, we have to catch up to the others and get registered. I tried texting you. What happened to getting some rest?" He glanced around the corridor, empty for the moment except for them and a thin woman in a sweater dress hanging a sign beside one of the rooms. "What are you doing over here, anyway?"

"Um...I got a little misdirected when I came downstairs. Turns out I couldn't rest after all." She gave him her best smile. "Too excited."

He looked at her skeptically. She knew the look well, had seen it on his face any number of times when he expected to pull her out of yet another jam.

Maybe this was going to be a little more difficult than time management.

Jenn didn't get lost. She never had in all the time he'd known her. Despite the number of times he and Connor had gone to rescue her, none of them had been because she couldn't find her way. She'd changed her clothes. And she was toting around that ridiculous bag again. The weight of it pulled her top tight, and he visually traced the curve of her bra before he caught himself. "Don't you think you should have left this in the room? Security will have a fit if you try to get to the tables with a suitcase on your back." He gave her a grin.

Her eyes lit up like he'd given her the best present ever, and he shivered. A look like that could mean a lot of trouble. The girl had an idea. And that usually meant something scary. Not to mention that it sent his blood rushing southward. Lord help him, he loved that look.

"Yeah, you're right. I better go take it back to the room. I'll meet you at the registration table in a few minutes."

"I'll walk with you. What have you got in there, anyway?"

She frowned. "You should never ask what's in someone's bag. A girl doesn't just give her secrets away. And I can walk by myself. You'd better go tell Connor I'll be a few minutes."

"Jenn—"

"Go on. I'm going to stop at the hotel desk to ask for more towels anyway." She started to walk away.

"The main desk is the other way."

She glared at him. That was even cuter than her here-comes-trouble look. "I can find my way just fine. Now you better go tell my brother I'll be along in a bit."

She wasn't going to let anything happen other than what she'd decided to do. He knew her well enough to understand that, just as well as he knew she'd probably decided on some mischief. He sighed. "Fine."

"Fine." She stared at him a minute longer.

She'd obviously taken a minute to blow dry her hair when she'd changed. Static had caught it, and she looked the tiniest bit possessed. He pressed his lips together and did his best to hide his amusement. She might kill him where he stood if she thought he was laughing at her. When she turned, his laughter died a quick death anyway—the curve of her ass in the deceptively plain skirt nearly brought him to his knees.

She walked away, and he leaned against the wall. This was never going to work. He wanted her; she'd always wanted him, even if she was pushing him away this week-end. If he broke down and let her know what she did to him, would she stop pushing and ask him in? The way she'd looked when she asked for mouth-to-mouth said something a lot different than the brush-off she'd just handed him. But he couldn't do the whole love 'em and leave 'em with her. Not Jenn. He'd never had a long-lasting relationship. His father had left his mother, and his father's father had left his grand-mother. What chance did he have with Jenn, when he was made with the kind of DNA that pushed men to wander?

She strode down the hall. Men. Always pushing a girl around. Even Adrian. She stormed around the corner and stopped short. The romance conference registration desk was open! She hurried over and quickly registered, confirmed her editor appointment, and collected her name tag, conference program, and a heavy bag stuffed with swag. She took a peek and nearly wiggled in excitement. Free books, stickers, leaflets, magnets, pins, pens and more. The program pamphlet drew her attention and the list of attendee names seemed to go on forever. There had to be time in her crazy schedule to get a good look at it all.

She walked toward the elevator. Her back was going to give out if she didn't drop off everything before she went to meet the boys. Besides, could she get any more obvious than a giant black shoulder bag that had a dozen author names on one side and a print of a kinky pair of handcuffs on the other? All she needed was a feather boa. No way could her brother mistake her swag bag for anything other than what it was.

Out of the corner of her eye, she caught the unmistakable shade of her brother's auburn hair. *Shit!* What was he doing away from the poker tourney already? Registration hadn't taken her more than a few minutes. Where could she hide? Why were they always following her? She ducked in front of a group of ladies headed back toward the romance side of the hotel. Good God, just because they *thought* they had to constantly rescue her... Okay, so yes, she'd had a bad year. There was the car wreck and the jerk of a guy she'd had to ditch, but she was a big girl, for goodness sake!

"Oh, you got your goody bag already! Is registration open?" One of the ladies behind her spoke up, and she had to look back. Adrian and Connor still stood near the elevator, but were scanning the lobby, clearly looking for her. Connor had his phone out, and she felt hers buzz with a text.

"Um, yeah. They opened early."

"I can't wait to see what they have this year. I loved last year's books. I hear there's more indie stuff out this year. I'm Nancy Clarke."

Recognition dawned. "Nancy? It's me, Jenn Riley!" She'd met Nancy online during a course she'd hosted and hit it off, but somehow it was harder to recognize her in person, despite the number of times she'd seen her picture.

Nancy smiled and pulled Jenn in for a quick hug. "I can't believe I ran into you so early. Come with us—after we get registered, we're going to a pre-con party. Everyone's going to be there."

"Really?" Excitement flooded her, taking her attention away from her brother and Adrian for just a minute.

"Oh, yes. I forget you're a conference virgin! The parties are the best places to meet people. Even Nora Roberts makes an appearance or two." She hooked Jenn's arm with hers. "Don't forget, you have to come to my class for first timers—I hold it every year. It's tomorrow morning, first thing."

Jenn smiled. "Sounds perfect." The poker tourneys never started before the afternoon since they went late into the night. She glanced back to where she'd seen her brother. He had his back to her but Adrian was looking right at her. Shit.

"I'm sorry I can't go tonight though." More sorry than she could say. "I have to go, I'm sorry. I...ah..." She wracked her brain. How the heck was she going to get past Connor and Adrian with her swag? "Do you know if there's a coat check or anything around here? And another set of elevators?"

Nancy gave her a look. "Not on this side of the hotel. You are staying here, right?"

"Yes...my brother and his buddies are here for the poker tourney and they invited me to come and I said yes but I really wanted to come to the romance convention so I snuck over here and now they're looking for me and I don't want to get caught because they will never quit poking at me until they read my book and my brother's best friend is the hero." Jenn took a deep breath.

Nancy's eyebrows had lifted higher on her forehead with every twist of her unending sentence. "Now that's a new one. I like it." She grinned. "Give me your bag, and I'll bring it to the class tomorrow. Just make sure you come early."

Jenn didn't hesitate. What the hell. "I hate to ask, but can you take this too?" She pulled her clutch purse out of her shoulder bag and handed both the bag with her manuscript and the swag bag over.

Nancy didn't look as amused, but she took both. Jenn

gave her a quick hug. Thank God it was Nancy and not a complete stranger. Before she could say anything else, Jenn realized her brother was on the move, and she made a quick goodbye. A cold sweat slipped along her back. What was she doing? She'd just given her book to someone she only knew online. Her book! But Connor catching her wasn't an option. If Connor found out about her writing, he'd want to read the book, and she hadn't changed it yet, hadn't changed the names and made it *not* Adrian and *not* Jenn having sex on so many pages. Bloody man. This was all his fault. His and Adrian's. Why hadn't Adrian just told her brother to wait for her?

She rushed through the side corridor. Thanks to her last escape, she had a good idea how to navigate behind the main lobby and reach the other side. She made it to the bar while their backs were turned and slipped inside. She needed a good drink, maybe two. Just to calm down before she went to register for the poker tourney. This whole thing was getting complicated, and she'd only arrived less than two hours ago.

"Grey Goose and cranberry, please." She took a seat at the bar, grateful that some of the earlier crowd had dispersed and left her room. The bartender returned a moment later, and she gave the drink a quick stir, then took a good gulp. Sweet with a bite, the vodka hit the spot. She took a look around. While she was here, maybe she should mingle. Just for a minute. It's not like being late for the tourney registration would matter—it would be open for four hours, for Pete's sake. There were no match games tonight, just practice ones people used to scout the competition. And she'd already turned down a party with *the* Nora! Wasn't that dedication enough? A likely group of probable authors sat in a small grouping of sofa and chairs at the edge of the bar. Nope, too close to the edge of the bar area. Connor would spot her for sure.

Speaking of him, she checked her phone. Yup, three texts.

Where are you?

We need to get registered

Brad's already got a practice game set!

Crap. Well, there wasn't much going on with the writers for the rest of the day, anyway, at least not without an invitation. The thought was a sour one, considering she'd already turned down an invitation to writer's heaven. At least she was registered for the romance conference. Time to work on goals two and three. Poker and Adrian. She took a gulp of her drink. Hello, liquid courage.

Chill big bro. Stopped in bar for a drink, come over.

His reply came in the form of one hot, hot man striding through the bar and right up to her.

"Connor's going to register and wants us to join him there. What are you up to, Jenn?"

"Just sitting here, having a drink." She waived the bartender over. "A Jack Daniels on the rocks for my sexy friend here."

"Jenn…" He took a seat, but she could see the reluctance in his posture.

"What, I can't enjoy myself here in Vegas? It is Vegas, Adrian. Let loose a little. The tournament doesn't start until tomorrow. Tonight we'll play some cards just for fun, have a good time." She touched his leg lightly and gave him her best come-hither look, lashes lowered. *Take the hint, Adrian.* Her heart beat a little harder when his gaze met hers and held.

When the bartender dropped off their drinks, she laid a few bills on the counter and took a long sip of her dark red drink. Adrian picked up his and rocked the amber liquid over the large ball of ice before tipping it back for a drink. He didn't acknowledge her hand on his leg, so after a second she took it back and sighed. Maybe hints weren't enough.

CHAPTER THREE

JENN'S TOUCH burned almost as much as the whiskey.
Or maybe it burned more—frankly, it was hard to decide, or
think at all, as all the blood in his brain rushed immediately
to his crotch. He didn't move, and eventually she took her
hand back and tossed down the fancy little drink. God,
what a mess. Considering her flirting, she still wanted him
and he wanted her, but it would be stupid to do anything
and end up hurting her. And he would.

"Jenn, this isn't a good idea. You know that."

"What happens in Vegas—"

"Might hurt you." He could tell he already had. Neither
was coming out and saying what was between them—they
hadn't said anything directly in the past, no matter how
much he'd wanted to. Especially the last time when he'd
desired so much more than a kiss. Every day for at least a
month he had debated going to see her at her college before
he'd regained control over himself.

She stood. "You finish up. Take your time. I'll go catch
up to Connor."

"All right. See you in a few." He'd give her some space to let it go and forgive him for not taking her up on her flirtations, like she always did. He couldn't stand up anyway, not without letting her know just how turned on he really was.

Of course she'd never gone too far with her flirting. Just tested the waters occasionally, checking the limits of how far he'd let her go. She probably didn't want him nearly as much as he'd like to have her, but he was strong enough, for her sake, to say no. But she was acting weird, even for Jenn, with all this running back and forth. He'd thought she'd be as into the tournament as Connor—it was her first after all, and after her car accident she could use the funds. That was probably the main reason she'd come on the trip, hoping to win some cash. There was always some scheme in play with Jenn, although they normally didn't have anything to do with money. Usually it was about boys, and he'd been the butt of more than a few of her pranks. That made him smile. He'd looked forward to her antics as a teen. They'd been fun—she'd been fun—and it felt good to be the focus of attention of someone so special.

He took a last sip of whiskey. Nice stuff. He narrowed his eyes, thinking about Jenn's dash away from him earlier in the corridor. What was she up to? She hadn't even finished her drink, though maybe she'd thought better of it if they were going to play poker. Time to go see. He nodded to the bartender and headed for the tournament rooms. A few minutes later he'd finished registering, the line having shortened considerably while he'd been in the bar. He spotted Jenn's name not too far above his on the check-in. That would satisfy her brother. Connor had joined Brad, and they were lounging casually at a table with a few professional players, Zoe Stratton included. Adrian grinned. Brad didn't give up easily.

Jenn was alone at a table dedicated for poker lessons. Adrian's grin faded. Although he couldn't hear her, it was easy to see the light, amused attitude she was giving the dealer. She leaned over the table, probably giving the man a good, if unintentional, view of the same low-cut yellow top Adrian had admired earlier. His stomach gave a twist. She had another drink beside her, her favorite from the dark red color, but she'd barely touched it. Knowing her routine, she'd probably left out the vodka now that she was sitting down to play.

He walked to her table in time to hear her give a sweet, deep laugh that had his balls tightening again. Jenn had zero use for poker lessens. She was kick-ass at the game and could probably go pro if she really wanted, just like Connor. So why play with the dealer?

"Can I join in?" Adrian took a seat to her left.

The dealer's eyes flicked from his to Jenn, then he shrugged. "Lady's choice."

Adrian held back a scowl. Of course it wasn't ladies choice—the tournament wasn't open yet, and anyone could get a practice game in. The learner and the practice tables were open to anyone. The dealer clearly wanted a beautiful player like Jenn to himself. Too bad.

"Oh, I supposed we can let him play," Jenn joked, but her voice was lower than usual, husky. "He's here with my brother, after all." Great. Way to imply he wasn't important. Then he caught the sideways look she gave him before she laughed. Played again. He joined her laughter.

The dealer took up his spiel. "The lady is skipping the usual Texas Hold'em tonight in favor of practicing her seven-card stud. No wildcards, and there's no ante, since this is a learner's table."

"But we *have* to bet with something." Jenn leaned toward Adrian. "How about we bet the winner's choice?"

The dealer frowned. At the learner's table, the dealer dealt himself a hand of cards to better help explain the game to new players. Winner's choice was a game Adrian had played with Jenn more than once and usually led him to doing something stupid. Like giving her a foot rub. Jenn was a better player than him, after all. But the dealer didn't get it. Adrian ground his teeth together. He had to put a stop to this.

Adrian waved at the dealer's deck. "Let's just play this round."

"Fine." Jenn sighed and watched as the dealer dealt them all three cards—two face down and one up.

Adrian checked his cards. Pure crap. Hopefully this wouldn't be a sign for how the weekend was headed for him. Jenn looked at hers and smiled, no poker face for her tonight. "The lady has the lowest door card. If we were betting, she would begin the bet." The dealer grinned at her.

She laughed. "I'd up my bet, if we were betting."

The dealer—Joe, according to his name tag—dealt their fourth card face up. A slight improvement for Adrian. The dealer had a deuce. Jenn had a face card, and her smile grew broader as Joe announced she had high card for the turn and would be the one leading the bet. *Great.* She crossed her legs in that little gray skirt, and he turned his gaze sternly back to his cards as the dealer dealt again.

Fifth, sixth, and seventh street didn't bring him much luck. He had a mess of cards with only a pair to show. Joe wore a permanent smirk and Jenn had a plate full of faces. She smiled at him, her eyes seeming to say exactly what he was thinking. That she was going to win, and that it might be a lot more than just this hand of poker.

"Show your hands." Joe flipped his cards over. A pair of deuces and a king.

At least he beat the smarmy dealer with a pair of nines and an ace. Jenn, of course, smoked them both. A lovely straight flush on the high end. When she wiggled in her seat, Adrian couldn't help smiling. She'd always been fun to play with, but now it was hard to ignore that she was damn sexy to play with, too.

And that led to all sorts of wrong thoughts.

"Let's play again." Jenn laughed. "Better luck next time." She casually reached over and patted Adrian's thigh.

She was flirting again. Not with the dealer, but with him. And not their silly flirting like in years past. She was treading a dangerous line. How much more could he take? His years-long infatuation had always been worse than her girlish crush, stronger and more dangerous for both of them.

Joe gathered the cards and shuffled out a new hand. With no bets being placed, the game took little time. In minutes Jenn had them beat again, this time with four of a kind. Luck was on her side. Too bad the tournament hadn't started. Joe gathered the cards, but Jenn fidgeted in her chair. Adrian knew the signs—she was feeling her luck and about to push it. He felt a little tug at his belly. Stopping didn't sound nearly as fun as staying and playing more with her. Even if he wasn't completely sure if he could stop it if she took things a step further.

Dangerous indeed.

"Let's bet after all," he said, although frankly he had no idea what he was doing.

"Goody." She smiled at the dealer. "What do you think, Joe? Does he have some unknown chance of winning?"

"I really can't speculate." Joe grinned back. "Shall I deal?"

"Okay, but the ante for him is the promise of a kiss. You're playing at the big table now, Adrian." She looked completely innocent, or she probably would if you didn't know her like he did. She glanced at him out of the corner of her eye.

Oh yes, he was in huge trouble.

Joe laughed at her bet. But he also told her he couldn't join in. Fine with her, since she wasn't interested in playing with the man. She looked at Adrian, who glowered back. "That's the ante, still going to play?"

"Fine." He practically growled it, and a thrill shot straight down her back. He knew what she wanted, no question there, but at least she'd gotten him to play along.

Joe handed out the cards, two down, one up. Seven-card stud was a game she'd loved since she was a kid and played with her father and brother for M&Ms. Now the stakes were so much higher. She had to make Adrian see her as a woman, not his friend's kid sister. She checked her cards. A pair of eights. Face up she had a six card. The dealer had the low card, so they'd skip this round of betting. Adrian kept his scowl, and she couldn't tell if that meant he had a good hand or bad.

Joe laid out the fifth street. Another eight! No way was she losing tonight. He was going to have to ante up, and she was going to kiss him, really kiss him. He wouldn't see the kid she'd been after that. She grinned.

"Better not smile like that in the tournament. You won't last five minutes." Adrian smirked, and her stomach dropped. Did he have better cards after all? He had the high card.

"What's your bet?" Joe asked, clearly amused by the whole thing.

"No betting after all—a kiss is quite enough," Adrian said, staring straight at her.

What the hell did that mean? He was messing with her. Or maybe still trying to protect her. "Fine. No betting, just the ante. Deal again."

Joe laid out the sixth street. He was quieter now, still amused by the smile on his face, but clearly aware there was something going on here and he wasn't going to get involved. "Lady has high card."

Three of a kind. She bit her lip and caught herself jiggling her leg. Adrian was right, she'd have to be calmer at the real games, but in a way, the stakes were higher here.

Joe dealt the final round. Nothing, but it didn't matter. "Show your hands." He flipped his two face-down cards. "House has two pair, threes high."

Jenn flipped hers. "Three eights." She smiled triumphantly at both Joe and Adrian. This was going to be her time, time for change.

"Not so fast. Straight flush." Adrian flipped his cards. All hearts, of course—two, three, four, five, six.

Dammit. Now she'd never collect on the ante, so what was the point of playing?

"Well, that's it for me, boys. The jetlag really has caught up with me, and I am going to turn in for some rest. Tomorrow's going to be a busy day." She slid from the tall chair. Adrian frowned at her. Well, if he was going to be cranky, she was going up to her room. All that good flirting wasted. But on the other hand, if she settled in for the night, she could have another look at her book pitch. And she had her netbook, so she could maybe work on the sequel…

Adrian caught her by the elbow. "I'll walk you to your room."

She glanced over at Joe, who looked at her with raised eyebrows. Cheeky dealer. Probably thought she was about to get laid.

If only.

CHAPTER FOUR

JENN HESITATED and Adrian tugged her elbow. "Let's go, Batgirl."

"Batgirl." She laughed, couldn't help it really. She hadn't heard that one in a while. He'd taken to calling her that when she was twelve and her mom had bought her a Batgirl raincoat. She'd hated the bloody thing, and he'd teased her more for it. That was when she first felt a little more for him than hero worship, although it was more obsession mixed with frustration than a crush. Just like right now.

"I haven't heard that one in a while." Was he trying to remind them of their childhood? That had been a fun time for sure. But it had gotten more fun as she grew older. "Play nice. I liked it when you called me Sasha better."

He let her pull away but followed her as she wove between the poker tables. He'd called her Sasha on the night they'd kissed. That was her D&D name back then, when she'd played a super sexy assassin in the role-playing game. They rode to her floor in silence.

When she stepped out, he followed.

Why was he sticking to her like glue? Did he want to take her up on her flirts after all? Or maybe tell her privately she had to stop? Her heart raced but her stomach dropped. What did he want?

He followed her to her room, so once she got it open she left the door wide open.

He frowned. Lovely. She obviously expected him to come in. Bad idea. He'd just wanted to walk her up so she was safe. And make sure she wasn't mad at him for winning—although she was probably more annoyed he didn't have to ante up for that kiss. But Jenn was hard to resist. And a pouting Jenn? Impossible. He stepped inside and shut the door behind him.

She was sitting on the edge of the king-size bed, working on taking off her shoes. When the tight little gray skirt rode up her long legs, his throat tightened.

She worked the first shoe off and let it drop to the floor. Then she looked up at him and smiled. Everything else tightened, and she looked like she knew it, with that sly smile that just curved the edge of her lips.

She worked her other shoe off, but kept her gaze on his. When she stood and walked toward him, he swallowed hard.

"So, how about the kiss?"

"I won, so no ante."

"True, but what better time than now, before the tournament and everything gets started and we both get distracted? I want a kiss, Adrian. It's been a long time since we shared one." She stepped close, close enough that he could circle her with his arms if he wanted to.

Dammit, he wanted to.

Hell with it.

"What happens in Vegas stays in Vegas." Corny, but in this case, it was going to be true. One kiss, and then he was staying far from her.

She took that as a yes, and her eyes widened. She bit her lip—probably hadn't imagined he would actually take her up on her teasing. Well, she should learn a lesson about men. This time he edged closer to her and leaned down into her space. She was much smaller without her heels and seemed younger with her eyes so open like that.

But then she raised her face to his and touched her lips against his mouth. She smelled so good, and the warmth of her lips seemed to spread through him. He wrapped an arm around her, drew her closer. Was she warm like that every-where? Yes. Her soft curves molded to his and a small moan escaped her.

That was it. He deepened the kiss, brushed his tongue against hers and tasted her. Her scent enveloped him, and he could imagine what her skin would taste like. What her passion would feel like.

When she ran her hands down his back, he hardened. She had to feel his arousal. He had to touch her, needed more. He held her close and stroked her arm with one hand, then palmed her breast through her top and bra. Still not enough. Her eyes were dark as she looked at him through her lashes, the irises wide and pushing the chocolate brown back.

He broke the kiss and nipped her lower lip, then kissed along her jaw and down her neck. She tasted exactly as he had imagined—delicious. Her breath came in soft gasps, and she clutched his arms, arching under his touch. So responsive. He pinched her nipple through her clothes, rolled the tight point, and watched her shudder in response. The little sounds she made were driving him crazy.

Another sound caught his attention and he froze. They both glanced at the door separating her room from her brother's. A noise sounded as someone moved around Connor's room. A door shut, and a moment later a soft tapping sounded at the connecting door.

What was he doing? Connor was back and he and Jenn were frozen like two teens caught in a clinch on their parents' sofa. He pulled away from her. This was Connor's sister, and *his friend*. Jenn was five years younger. For a second, he imagined her as bitter as his granny or as broken as his mom. She didn't need that, didn't need *him*.

"Jesus."

She grimaced, clearly aware he was regretting the kiss going further than a peck on the lips. Her shoulders drooped, and she sighed when he stepped away. "Impeccable timing. I always knew I wanted to be an only child."

Good grief. The man was trying to kill her. Seriously, she might die from unfulfilled desire. Was that even possible? Her knees shook, and she flopped down on the bed before she went totally limp with need. God, she'd never had an issue with a man saying no before this. It wasn't like she'd never seduced a good looking guy, either. But Adrian wasn't just anyone, and she'd barely been able to keep her head on straight when he'd come in after her. She hadn't had any time to use her *moves*. Just to ask for a kiss.

And what a kiss. Hello.

And now he was gone, her brother was back and would

probably be a pest, and she didn't even have her book to look through or any of the conference goodies.

The knock came at her door again. Might as well answer and see what Connor was up to, or he'd keep on knocking until she did.

"Just a minute!" Jenn shimmied out of her skirt and sat up to pull off her top and throw on an old, extra large T. She grabbed a washcloth from the bathroom and wet it. Good thing she was familiar with the effect of a serious kiss on her makeup. And with snooping brothers. She started washing and went to the adjoining door, washcloth in hand.

She pulled open the door. Her brother looked surprised for a second, then walked right in and looked around.

"Hey. What's up?"

"Nothing. Decided to call it a night since Brad has only one thing on his mind and you and Adrian disappeared." He looked around. "Where is he, anyway?"

Jenn bit back her frustration. Her goals were not working out. Her book was MIA, well, not missing but not with her, the man of her dreams seemed determined to keep her at arm's length, and her bother just might be on his side —at least inadvertently. He certainly seemed to be in the way. All she had going was the poker.

"I don't know, probably his room. He walked me up here and left a bit ago." She walked to the mirror hanging on one wall and leaned close to take a look. Yup, good call on the washcloth. Her lips were totally smudged and a little swollen. Which made her think about the kiss...

"Hello? I said I hope he didn't head back down to Brad's table."

She looked back at him. "Sorry. Why's that?"

"Brad's definitely out to get laid tonight. The idiot."

Her stomach twisted. Adrian had left her here, all hot

and bothered, lips bruised and lady-parts aching. He'd better not be going out to get some. She squeezed the washcloth so hard it dripped on her foot.

Time for a change of subject. "How did you make out tonight? You got a couple of games in. You like the odds?" She went back to the bathroom and washed her face in earnest while Connor rambled about the players and his plan for domination. Little chance he'd win overall, not unless he'd recently taken to shoving horseshoes up his butt, but he could win big enough to be asked to join another tournament, and that seemed to be his current plan. Same as hers. She had to remember that part of her weekend plan —winning the ladies' tourney, or at least placing high enough to win some serious cash.

Eventually she shooed her brother out and settled down in bed with her netbook. She logged onto her cloud account and made sure her manuscript had backups on top of backups. Then she called the front desk and set up a wake-up call. No way was she missing the newbie class. She grinned as she set the phone back in its cradle. By getting up early, she'd be easily able to ditch the guys for a couple of hours and spend some quality time with her fellow writers.

CHAPTER FIVE

ADRIAN WAITED until the second round of the practice game he was having with Connor and a few other players to ask what he'd wanted to ask all morning. "So, where's Jenn?" The tournament was supposed to start in two hours, and she hadn't shown. Was she still mad about last night? He couldn't blame her. She couldn't have been happy about the way he took off. But clearly she hadn't said anything to her brother, who would have killed him by now if she had.

Connor kept his eyes on the game. "She's taking some poker lessons this morning. A kind of brush-up."

"You have to be kidding me. Jenn? She's a shark."

Connor shrugged. "Everyone has their routine."

Yeah, right. Jenn wasn't a tourney hound; she didn't have lucky rituals. And she sure as hell didn't need lessons. Sober, she beat him every time. Of course, that could be because it was getting harder and harder to keep his mind on the game with her around. He scanned the room. There were a lot of tables and a lot of people mingling, but he couldn't see her anywhere. Was she taking private lessons somewhere else?

Connor elbowed him in the side when he frowned. "That's quite a poker face. It's your bet."

"I fold." He nodded to the dealer and clapped a hand on Connor's shoulder before standing and walking away. He would not think about the surprise or the speculation he'd seen flash in his friend's eyes.

He'd just take a little walk around and see if he could find her. He couldn't let her stay mad at him, and apologizing was better done sooner rather than later with her.

That kiss... It was all he could think about last night. The way she'd pressed against him, so responsive, so sexy, so...perfect.

Too bad she couldn't say the same for him.

He strode out of the tournament area and past the entrance hall and the bar. No sign of Jenn and no notices posted for poker lessons. He headed for the main desk. They would probably have a listing of any practice rooms for the tournament. What was he doing anyway, going after her again? She wasn't a kid. Her brother wasn't worried. He should just leave her alone.

But what if she hated him for leaving her?

He couldn't let that happen.

Long legs and a familiar, slender figure caught his attention. Jenn stood at the far end of the hotel lobby, gathered with a bunch of women. What was she doing over there again? He glanced at the signage announcing the romance convention. A whole convention dedicated to romance books? Bizarre. Jenn smiled and laughed, then received a big hug from a complete stranger, or at least a stranger to him. She seemed to know these ladies well enough. He walked toward her.

"Excuse me, you're him, right?" A middle-aged woman with bright pink streaks in her hair touched him lightly on the arm, stopping him before he could reach Jenn. "You're Davis Jerome, the cover model from *inDelicate* and *Beautiful Lies*?"

At her words, a half dozen women flocked in his direction. He took a step backward. "Uh..."

"Oooh, can I take your picture with my group?"

"Are you signing copies later?"

"I love your abs. Can you give us a peek for the shot?"

"I'm sorry, I'm—"

Someone pulled up the corner of his shirt. Jeez. Good thing he had been working out lately. What the hell was happening here? "I'm sorry." He caught the edge of his shirt and pulled it down where it belonged. "I'm not Davis whoever and I'm not on the cover of any books. I'm just looking for a friend."

"Oh, I'm so sorry," the girl with the pink stripes apologized, but she looked more amused than put out by his revelation. "You sure should be on a cover though." She ginned impudently and patted his stomach.

"Ah, thanks?" He had to be three shades redder than her hair by now. The little crowd around him broke up, although a few continued to give him some speculative looks. He glanced around the lobby and down the hall, but got distracted as his phone began to vibrate with incoming texts.

Mom: What a mess. Your brother is home with me

Divorce not going well

She wants house and cottage and car and allowance!
Punishing him for sure

Call me when you are free

Perfect. More crap he'd have to deal with when he got

home. His brother probably *was* being punished. Then again, he probably hadn't kept it in his pants. Typical. And a good reminder of the predilections that ran in the family genes. He looked around again at all the women gathered for the romance convention. A lot of effort to put out on a silly dream. That was what romance was.

Where was she? Jenn was gone again. What the hell was she up to?

Jenn tossed her bags on the bed, and the heavy manuscript pages slid out, held together with a thick, black bulldog clip. Her brain was buzzing, and for a moment she flopped on the bed beside the bags and lay back flat. What a fantastic morning! It was hard to say if she was exhilarated or scared to death, though. The workshop on character development had her doubting whether she'd put enough motivation into her characters, but it was a bit late now—she'd confirmed her appointment with an editor to pitch the book for tomorrow afternoon.

She wrapped her arms around herself and laughed. The first class of the morning had been hilarious—Nancy was right, she'd needed the workshop for newbies. The social rules around what she should and shouldn't do were so obvious. She felt like an idiot for not realizing them before now. Thank God, they told her she could stop carrying the manuscript around, that no editor or agent would ever want to schlep it home. *Duh.* Her back was killing her from carrying it all morning. But at least she had it back. She'd had no idea of the stress she'd been carrying around with it gone until she had it back in her hands again. She picked up the papers and pulled off the clip, then through to her favorite scene, the ending.

She'd written everything down she'd ever wished for from Adrian. Even used his and her names as a sort of cathartic way to try and purge the crush she'd had for years. She'd change that, of course, before it was published. At first, using the names had felt odd, like she was writing in her diary, but then it got easier and the words just spilled out of her. The thoughts, dreams, fantasies. The super hot fantasies. Taking the names out later would be weird. This was her story, what she wished it would be between her and Adrian. If nothing else, writing it all down had really made it clear she needed to give him one last chance. This weekend was it. And damn if that kiss hadn't been a good start.

She looked at the clock and groaned.

Much as she wanted alone time with him, it was hard not to resent the fact she had no chance of attending the afternoon sessions of the romance conference. There were some really good writing workshops happening that could help her a lot. But she'd promised to meet the guys for dinner and then go to the early bird games for the tournament. That part of her weekend goal, playing for money, had already started to look far less appealing than when she'd first come up with this whole scheme. But she'd promised, so she sat up and stretched, rolled her head around on her neck and then stood to check her appearance in the mirror. Not bad for having zero sleep. Damn Adrian. She headed for the door. Time to meet up with the man who'd kept her up all night, and not in a fun way.

Five minutes later, Jenn took her seat between her bother and Brad and opposite Adrian at the four-person table in the dining room.

"How were poker lessons?" Adrian gave her a look when he asked. He definitely suspected something. What a snoop. A sexy one, but still. It wasn't like she was going to die when they found out about her writing. But it was nice to have a chance to savor the experience, before they teased her unmercifully.

"Oh, they were good, a nice brush-up before today's games. But I admit I did sneak away to do a little shopping." There. A pretty good cover. What kind of guy didn't believe a girl would want to hit the shops in Vegas? One of Adrian's eyebrows rose toward his hairline.

That kind of guy, evidently.

"I'm surprised you made it back here on time. There must be a lot of shops around," Adrian said. He was fishing.

"Oh, it was hard to leave, believe me. What are you having for lunch, Connor?" She stared pointedly at her menu. "Everything looks great, and I can't decide."

Adrian kept at her. "I really wouldn't have thought you'd need lessons."

Okay, he was *not* letting this go. "Ah, well. A girl has to stay sharp. Not like she can wait around on some guy to keep her entertained." *There.* Chew on that one. She watched the little muscle in his jaw jump. A muscle she'd love to kiss. Then his neck, then—

"Well, you have your work cut out for you in the ladies' tournament," Brad interjected. "There're some sharp players here."

"Checking them out for speed last night, weren't you, Brad?" Connor jumped in with a grin on his face.

Jenn stifled a sigh of relief. The discussion would continue and linger on what Brad had been up to and not on her questionable activities. Except Adrian was looking at her. Staring. She could feel it and, damn, if her nipples didn't harden at the thought. She had it bad.

Lunch passed quickly. All the cloak-and-dagger running around, making sure nobody caught her taking lessons on writing hot sex scenes or anything else at the conference, had made her hungry.

"Crap, I forgot my pass in your room." Adrian nudged Connor with his elbow. "Give me your key, and I'll go grab it."

Her brother fished his key card out and handed it over. Jenn shook her head. Here she was, imagining he was watching her, thinking about her, and he had his mind on the game, as always.

"Put my lunch on my room tab, will you?" Adrian asked the group in general as he stood. He brushed by her without catching her glance, and she slumped in her seat. He was driving her crazy and probably had no idea.

Jenn was driving him crazy. His poker game was going to be crap if he couldn't even keep his thoughts straight enough to remember his pass. She was at the root of it, or maybe it was simply the temptation to give in to his baser side and have a Vegas affair with her. He wanted to. She seemed to want him to. But where would that leave them afterward?

He keyed Connor's room open and walked inside. His pass lay on the corner of the dresser, although he really couldn't remember leaving it there. Again, his brain was mush. The other little brain was trying to take over. The one in his pants.

The door between the adjoining rooms was just slightly open. Another temptation.

He shouldn't look. He should just go back down and try to get his head in the game. But he could smell a hint of her perfume. It wouldn't hurt anything to look—well, except his willpower. It could absolutely hurt that. Still, he stepped through and looked around her room. He was pathetic.

The place was a bit of a mess, but not bad. Not like her brother's room. Good God, the guy had only been here one night, and it looked like a tornado had ripped on through. Jenn's bags lay on the bed, some stuff spilled out. He walked to the bed and tried very, very hard not to look at the discarded silk teddy on the pillow. Tried just as a hard not to sniff at the lingering scent of her in the room.

Who was he kidding? He breathed in deep. What the hell was he going to do? He couldn't get involved with Jenn and wreck their friendship. It was too special. Already she was torn between flirting with him like always and avoiding him. If he hurt her, she would never forgive him.

One of the bags on the bed was black canvas with a bunch of sponsor names on the side. Pamphlets lay in piles beside it and a magazine. And...another poker tournament badge? She must have forgotten hers too. He picked it up and flipped it over. Nope. A romance conference ID. He stopped, stared at the badge with her name on it. *Oooookay...*

He sat on the edge of the bed as relief rushed though him. The sponsor bag on her bed. The pamphlets. This was what she'd been up to. The minx was secretly attending the romance convention. A bit of tension eased from his shoulders. At least she wasn't really avoiding him. She probably didn't want to get razzed for the next year by her brother for going. And maybe him. He grinned. Definitely him. He was so going to tease her over this one.

He stood. Time to go back to the restaurant before

someone came looking for him. When he pushed away from the mattress, the pile of papers and pamphlets shifted, and although he made a grab for it, the whole mess of them went over the edge. Shit.

He walked around and collected everything, put the pamphlets back in a few piles as best as he could remember how they'd been before. He picked up the sheaf of papers in a loose bulldog clip and flipped through it.

He sucked in a breath.

Adrian stared at the pages in his hand. The black clip fell to the floor from his weakened fingers. His name appeared again in the crisp, typed font. This time on the heroine's lips. He damn near dropped the papers, so he sat down hard on the chair by the window. He'd stopped breathing and needed some air. Jesus.

"Adrian, can you help me with this zipper?"

Jenn turned away from him, waiting. What choice did he have? How could he say no when he wanted to help her undress. The single step between them disappeared, and he slid the zipper down her back to where he expected to see the back of her bra, to where she would be able to reach it. But there was no bra line. Adrian pulled the zipper farther until suddenly he was at the small of her back. His heart slammed in his chest, and he froze, then took a step back. He hadn't meant to go so far...

She shifted, slipping her arms from the sleeves. The dress slid down her hips slightly with the motion, and his gaze focused on the slim line of bare skin at the base of her back. She wasn't wearing any panties, either. His cock pulsed, hardened, and he swallowed hard.

Then she dropped the dress entirely.

He nearly went to his knees, driven by the sight of her

long neck, the line of her spine, the curve of her sweet ass. Every inch of her exposed and free for his touch.

She glanced over her shoulder, her usually mischievous eyes now big, dark, smoldering. "Adrian."

His name was enough invitation. "Jennifer." He said her name, reached for her, touched—

The paper slipped from his fingers. Where the hell was the next page? Jesus. He couldn't, *shouldn't* read this. Jenn had written this. About him. And her. And...doing... His cock throbbed in his pants. What the hell was he supposed to do about this?

Jenn wanted him. The kiss they'd shared had made it clear how much. He'd known it for a while, but this certainly drove home the point. And the evidence of his returned desire throbbed right there in his pants. But he couldn't let it happen. Not with his history. He couldn't do that to her. His father had left his mother. And his grandfather, his father's father, had left his wife, too. His brother was in the middle of a messy divorce. It ran in the genes. Men in his family just couldn't do commitment.

He looked down at the scattered pages. She'd written an entire fantasy about them. What was she doing, carrying around a...book like this? When he started to gather up the pages, it dawned on him. Hello, it was a *book*. He froze. His stomach tightened. She had an entire book, a sexy book, about *him*, and she was attending a romance convention. *To sell it.* Great.

What was he going to do? Clearly, she had more than a little crush on him, and having gone this far, all the way to writing out an entire fantasy, she wasn't about to let it go. And after the kiss they'd shared last night, he didn't really want to, either. Maybe if they got this out of their system now, had a little affair in Las Vegas where nothing was really real, she could accept it when he moved on. He'd have to move on. Staying just wasn't in his genes.

He picked up another page and glanced at it, sucked in his breath at the heat written out in black and white. This was definitely coming with him up to his room. She'd kill him if she knew he'd been snooping, but no way was he leaving the book here for her to sell to some stranger to publish for the world to see. Not before he read it. The whole thing too, not only the hot parts, although those would probably give him a heart attack.

Jenn was undeniably all grown up. Maybe...maybe they could have a little something together without anyone breaking any hearts. After all, what happened in Vegas stayed in Vegas.

CHAPTER SIX

FIVE HOURS LATER, and Adrian's mind was still on the papers he'd put in his room to finish reading later. He hadn't been able to stop himself from reading more before he put them in his nightstand, and the chapter he'd consumed had nearly made him late for the first round of the tournament. Well, not quite true, cleaning up after he'd released some of the pressure in his blue balls after reading the chapter had nearly made him late. He'd had no idea romance books could be that intense.

He took his seat at the table for his fifth game. He was doing all right, but not great. So it was mere luck that he got to sit at Jenn's table now in a mixed round. She'd won two hands and lost one, but stayed at her table as a winner in the last round, chalking up points in the women's division. When he sat two seats down from her, he realized she seemed distracted, barely glancing at the new players around her.

She probably wanted to be at the romance convention. Then why had she bothered to come to the poker tournament? Because her brother needed a fourth for the team? Or because of him? The idea made him harden, but it also brought a brisk pace to his heart that didn't bode well. Was it excitement or terror that had his chest pounding? Hell, on the other hand, maybe she just came because Connor paid for the flight and the room. She didn't make a lot at her job, although she never seemed broke. How much did writer's make, anyway? Would she make a lot off her hot little book? *Their* hot little book. It was about the two of them. Her writing made his heart pound. She was really, really good. At one time, he would have made fun of her for writing smut. But her writing was more than that. It made him feel...something. And not just the bulge in his pants.

He laid out his hand and watched as the dealer announced the win—neither he nor Jenn were going to get much farther in the tournament if they didn't start paying attention. But it hardly seemed fair she might sell a book starring their sexual exploits when they hadn't even had any. Maybe his thought about Vegas and the crazy stuff that happened here was for real. Maybe it was time to up the ante. She was clearly all grown up and making good use of her fantasy life. If she was going to use him for inspiration, she had to know that not everything ended up in a happy-ever-after.

As long as he was really clear with her on that, he was all in.

He was staring at her, again. She could feel it. No way was she looking at him to check, though. No way.

Okay, she looked, and his hot stare made her gulp.

He'd barely said a word since he sat down—not that there had been much opportunity since the poker hands at this level went faster. But he kept *looking*. Not teasing, not flirting, just watching her. Was he thinking about their kiss? Did he want more or want her to back off? So far this trip held nothing more than frustration. Not enough time to take all the writing classes she was interested in, not enough time to get into the game, and not enough time alone with Adrian.

"Hand to Lady Rose."

Gah. Her game was sadly off. She should have won. Players who effected personas like "Lady Whatever" should not be on the winning side of a deck of cards. The cameras seemed to love it though. The tourney was being filmed—nothing new, she'd signed the regular waiver—and people seemed to be treating it like a reality show. Lovely.

"That's it for me, folks." Jenn stood. "I'm calling in my time limit for tonight. It's been a long day."

Lady Rose looked at her with what had to be disdain. "Yes, you do look tired. Absolutely pale and wrung out like an old dishcloth. Best go get some rest, bless your heart." She laid the Southern accent on thick, and the insult was as sweet as pie.

Spare me. "Lovely theatrics. See you all tomorrow."

It was tempting to stay a little longer and wipe the grin off the heavily made-up poker bitch. But there was no use, she wasn't into it, and not even playing along against a wanna-be Southern poker belle was going to keep her from going back to her room and crawling in with her iPad writing program. She might as well go over her pitch for the editor one more time. It was too late to sneak over for anything more at the writing con—only the private parties would still be happening at this time of night, and she was just too pooped for that. Not to mention not in the mood, even if Nancy had told her about how fun they could be and the amazing people she could meet. Socializing took a cheerful energy she didn't think she had in her, at least not at the moment.

She risked a glance at Adrian, but he was staring at Lady Rose. Nice. Well, whatever. She headed for the hall, signed out at the door, and walked to the elevator. Maybe he liked the man-killer look.

Five minutes later, and she was gratefully kicking off her shoes in her room. The carpet squished under her toes, and she heaved a sigh of relief. The light was off, probably something housekeeping did, so she walked through and flipped the light switch by the door and the bathroom, then went to the window and pulled the drapes closed. It wasn't really that late—only just past ten, but it had been a long day. A shower sounded heavenly. She walked back to the bathroom, stripping off as she went, and turned on the hot water.

She frowned as she climbed into the shower. It felt like she was forgetting something, or as though there was still something she should be doing, but what? God knew there was enough on her plate. She'd made the tourney and got in enough games to qualify. She'd registered for everything at the writing conference she'd be able to fit in around the tourney. Adrian was a wash for now. So what?

Hot water poured down her back while she soaped her hair. She rinsed and stepped out onto the bathmat to grab a towel and then stood still, dripping. Something was missing. She wrapped the towel around her and trotted out to the bed. Her piles of conference loot spilled across the lower half of the bed in loose heaps.

When she sat on the edge of the bed, some of the goodies slopped over as she tilted the mattress. Her heart pounded. She lifted the empty conference bag. Nothing.

She had to be crazy; imagining things. She stood and walked around the bed. Nothing. No piles of paper. She glanced around the room. Nothing on the table by the window or the chair or the dresser.

"Oh, my God. Where the hell is my book?"

She rose and checked the garbage can. Empty. Could housekeeping have taken her book? Why would they? It had been on the bed, she was sure of it. She could remember slipping off the bulldog clip, looking through it, and then laying it on the bed before she headed out. Could someone else have been in her room? Her iPad lay on its case where she'd left it the night before. Her suitcase sat on the stand next to the dresser. She walked to it and flipped it open. Her camera lay inside. No one would steal a manuscript and leave an iPad and camera, would they?

A chill slid down her back. She walked to the door separating her room from her brother's. It wasn't quite shut.

"Oh. My. God."

She clutched her towel tighter. Water dripped from her hair down her back, and she shivered in the air-conditioned room. She opened the connecting door and the second door. It was unlocked, and when she glanced into the mess that was her brother's room, nothing looked disturbed.

She had shut that door. Hadn't she? Someone had been in her room and taken her book after coming though her brother's room.

Heat spread from her cheeks until it felt like her whole body was on fire, wet hair or no. She walked back to her room. Was Connor reading her book right now? Or worse, Adrian? Oh, dear God, if either of them had it, she would never live through the embarrassment they would put her through. She flopped on the bed, and her body betrayed her, tingling at the thought of Adrian reading her book. Would it turn him on? It had to—it was practically porn in some places.

She groaned and put her hands to her head, holding the weight since her neck seemed ready to give in at the round of mortification that flooded her.

She took a deep breath and grabbed her purse from the nightstand. She searched through until she found her phone. Quickly she texted her brother, asking him if he was finished for the night. If he was still playing she'd have to wait. After a moment, her phone buzzed.

Yeah, done for now, going to bar. Want to come?

That sounded normal enough. But her brother could be tricky.

Nah, I'm beat

OK, see you. Don't be late tomorrow! Seen your scores and you need a few wins.

She couldn't ask anything else and tip him off that she was upset. He didn't sound like he wanted to make fun of her; ribbing her about her distracted game was typical.

OK. What about the guys?

Brad's with me, Adrian wimped out and crashed.

OK, night

She paced the room. Maybe housekeeping really did take it. Bu the room didn't look any different than when she'd been in it last, except the book was gone. So why would housekeeping have been in here? And it didn't seem to have been Connor... That left Adrian, or some crazed manuscript thief from the conference. It wasn't like she didn't have another copy; she had her copy on the iPad and on her laptop at home and backed up on the cloud. Her thoughts circled back to Adrian.

Adrian, reading her book. Her nipples tightened. Adrian, getting hot reading her book. Flipping through the pages and reading that one scene...oh, God. When heat flushed through her core, she crossed her legs, trying to relieve the tension as desire that rushed through her. The image of him, stroking himself and reading her words, nearly made her dizzy.

She was going to die.

After a minute, she sighed and got up. No way could she go to bed without knowing what had happened to her baby. That's what her book was. It had taken months to write the thing, revise it, and edit it. And if Adrian, who played a starring role in the story, had it, she needed to know. And she needed to know what he thought of it.

Jenn toweled off and threw on her yoga pants and a T-shirt. This wasn't the time to get dressed up in skirt and heels. She just had to get it over with. If he had it, she had to face him, find out what he thought, and either jump him or pay him off so he never told her brother. Like that was going to happen. He'd never be able to resist telling Connor she wrote smutty romance. Okay, jump him and *blackmail* him into never telling.

She headed for his room. If the idiot had taken the Southern belle wanna-be to his room, he was in for a rude awakening.

A quick elevator ride and a swift march down the hall and she was at his door. She hesitated. What if he didn't have the book? What would she say?

"Good grief. Take a chance, girl. That's what the weekend is about, for God's sake."

"Talking to yourself?" The deep voice came from behind her, and she nearly jumped three feet, straight up in the air. Adrian.

"You always sneak up on people?" She turned to face him. "I was just coming to talk to you." Her mouth dried.

He wore a pair of soft-looking, faded jeans and nothing else, no T-shirt, and just a pair of socks. His hair was wet from the shower, just like hers. *Yum.*

"Nope, but I did have to get some ice." A group of laughing people approached. As they walked by, he pressed closer to her to get out of the way. She could feel the heat pouring off all that glorious skin and muscle. He brushed past her and slid his key through the slot to open the door. Sure enough, he was carrying an ice bucket. She followed him into the room.

There was no mess in his hotel room, unlike her brother's. But there was no manuscript anywhere that she could see, either.

"What's up? I thought you left the table early to get some rest?"

He sounded so casual. How could he possibly sound like this if he had her book? Jenn pressed her lips together. He wasn't really looking at her when he spoke. Was that a sign of guilt?

"Couldn't you sleep? Something on your mind keeping you out of bed?"

She froze. His words...they were familiar. Too familiar. They were lines from her book. Lines right in the middle of the scene where he'd laid her on the bed and slid his hand under her skirt, only to find she wasn't wearing any panties. Could him repeating the line be coincidence? She licked her lips. How the heck was she going to do this? She looked around the room again.

"It's late, but I can't settle. Want to play a hand?" She waved her hand toward the card deck on his nightstand.

"Sure." He patted the edge of the bed and gathered up the cards. He shuffled, his gaze never leaving hers.

She followed every tiny movement, tracking the play of

his muscles in his forearms and biceps. Without a shirt, he was a piece of art. Sit on the bed and play cards with him? Oh yeah, definitely.

As he dealt, she collected her cards. A bland hand at best. The muscles in his chest had thickened since she saw him last, two months ago at her parents' home, wet from their backyard pool. She swallowed. Better find out soon if he'd read the book; she might jump him without knowing if she waited much longer.

"I'll take five."

He raised an eyebrow. She smiled and watched him watch her mouth. There was no noise from the hallway anymore, only the sound of both of them breathing and the soft shuffle of the cards as he dealt her a new hand.

"And make it a good hand this time."

He grinned. "You want a lot."

"I want it all."

He lost the grin, but his eyes darkened with a sexual look that made her heart beat faster. Yup! Dammit! He'd read the book. That was her line, from the same chapter as the bit he'd quoted about her not being able to sleep. She looked down at her cards, trying to decide what to do next. A full house. Now the cards were talking. "Call."

"We haven't bet anything yet," he said. His eyes were still dark, hungry. As she leaned forward, he sucked in a breath.

"How about we play for a favor? If I win, you owe me a favor. If you win, you can ask me for something."

He stared at her for a moment. He hadn't been able to stop himself from flirting, teasing her, with a couple of lines from her book. And then she gave him one back. She knew he'd read the book. Thank God, he'd put it back in the night-stand when he decided he needed some ice for the whiskey he'd snagged out of the minibar fridge. Otherwise she would have seen it on the bed and would have probably killed him by now. Things were getting out of control, fast.

And he couldn't bring himself to stop it. Didn't even want to try.

He looked down at his cards. A measly pair, despite his second draw. He really was a lousy dealer. "All right. A favor." She was going to win; he could see her tell. What would she ask for from him? The book, clearly. But it sure would be nice if she asked for something more. He'd been half-hard since he started reading the damn thing.

She smiled, a syrupy, I've-got-you-now smile. "Agreed." When she laid down her hand, he winced.

"Full house."

He laid down his rather pathetic pair of deuces. "You win. What do you want?" The last bit came out hard and a tad rough, but he couldn't bring himself to clear his throat when he really wanted to pounce on her, roll her over on the bed, and do every single thing she'd written about in chapter nine.

She leaned closer. "I want back what I lost," she whispered.

She wanted the book. Well, too bad. No way was he giving that back, not until he finished reading it, at least. Only one thing he could do. "Last night you lost a kiss." He closed the distance between them and kissed her. She could have back the kiss she'd lost. Light at first, then he slanted his head and took it deeper, reveling when she returned the pressure.

She opened to him, and he took the opportunity, raising the bet by licking her lips and sliding his tongue into her mouth. She tasted dark and delicious, like red wine, only better with something that was pure Jenn. He traced his fingers down her arms, then up her sides until he brushed the edge of her breasts. She shivered.

When he cupped her breasts through her T-shirt, they both moaned. She wasn't wearing a bra. He pulled away a bit, enough to break the kiss and look in her eyes. She stared at him, then leaned in for another kiss. That was invitation enough. He tilted back onto the bed and brought her with him, his cock thickening as the weight of her pressed against him. Cards slid everywhere, mostly to the floor. She straightened her legs, and the last bit of sanity he had fled as her yoga-pant covered heat fit perfectly over his cock.

If they'd stripped first, he would have taken her immediately and hard. Thank God, for denim. His jeans between them gave him pause enough to remember he had to do this right. It might be their only time, and he wanted—needed—to know he'd given her his best.

He kissed her again, or maybe she kissed him. He took his time tasting her, and she ground against him in response. This was going to take some willpower. But first, just to be clear...

"So there's only one way to say this. You know what happens in Vegas—"

"Stays in Vegas. Shut up and kiss me again." She was out of breath, and probably the best sight he'd ever seen, up on top of him like that, wild and willing.

He kissed her, and explored her breasts with both hands until she huffed in frustration and pushed his hands out of the way so she could pull off her T. *Damn.* Her breasts were beautiful, perfect and creamy with rosy tips. He leaned up on one elbow and took the end of her breast in his mouth, sucking her nipple hard. He palmed the other and kneaded her soft flesh. She moaned in encouragement and ran her hands over his chest to tease his nipples in turn. She pinched one, and he wrapped an arm around her and rolled them both over on the king-size bed so she was underneath him and the last of the poker deck had sailed to the floor.

He kissed her throat, her collarbone, her breasts. Then slid one hand down the delicate skin of her belly to the edge of her yoga pants. He ran his fingers over the seam of the material from hipbone to hipbone while he circled one of her nipples with his tongue. He drew her deeper into his mouth and slipped his hand under the material of her pants to find her pussy.

And damn near came when he realized she was panty-less and shaved clean.

She spread her legs wider in response. She was wet and steamy. He spread her lips and pressed a finger inside her. She shuddered. He found her clit and circled the little bud with his wet finger.

Everything was going fine until she grabbed his cock through his jeans and rubbed. Next thing he knew he was hauling her yoga pants down and pressing his fingers deep inside her. His own pants were down around his calves, and her hands were wrapped around his cock. It was a trade-off who was going to come first, this way, and he couldn't have that. No. Jenn had to get the very best of tonight. He slid down between her legs and sucked at her clit hard. She tasted like heaven. She shuddered. Again. And again, and then she arched her back and cried out in release.

A condom. Where the hell was his wallet? Oh yeah, in the pants that were tangling him up. He retrieved the packet and tore it open. *Jesus.* His cock might explode soon. He kicked off the jeans, got on his knees in front of her, and rolled it on. He took a long breath. She was making him lose his mind. He caught her legs in each hand. She bent her knees and folded them close to her chest, exposing her wet pussy. He centered himself and tried to slow his breathing as he pressed inside her.

It took everything he had not to pound into her but to take it slow and savor the moment, the intense pleasure of being completely engulfed in her. He set the pace, a slow one, *goddamnit*, and let go of one leg so he could stroke her clit. She looked dazed and whimpered and shuddered under him. With each thrust in, he circled her clit, until she tried to feebly push his hands away. Instead he picked up the pace and thrust harder, keeping up the circles with his wet thumb against her sensitive flesh.

"Adrian…" She moaned his name, and pleasure wound down through his spine, straight to his balls. "Adrian!"

He slammed into her and pinched her clit until she screamed, stiffening under him in a hard orgasm. He came too, hard enough to make his vision blurry.

She was everything he'd ever imagined.

Damn it.

CHAPTER SEVEN

WHATEVER THE HELL that God-awful sound was, she was going to kill it. She ached everywhere, in the most delicious way. And she wanted to sleep for a while. Maybe for a day or two. She sure hadn't gotten any sleep last night. Jenn grabbed her pillow, put it over her head, and considered the night's events. Adrian had given her more pleasure than she'd ever had in one night. They'd had sex until she could barely speak, never mind walk, although somewhere around four in the morning she'd slipped out of bed and pulled on her clothes and came to her room while he slept.

Why had she done that? The morning sex could have been soooo good. The man had a gorgeous cock, everything she'd imagined and a little more. And he sure as hell knew what to do with it. She grinned.

The noise wouldn't stop. She groaned and pulled her pillow off her head. The alarm clock crowed at her.

"Shit." She was so not a morning person. More than anything, she wanted to smash the alarm clock to hell, but it appeared she'd already hit snooze a few times. She rolled out of bed, her muscles aching. Once she was completely upright, she shut the alarm off. Then she stood, groaned, and headed for the bathroom. Once there, she looked in the mirror. Yup. This was why she'd left last night. She looked like she'd run a marathon in high winds—her hair stuck out everywhere. But, wow, she felt good. Used, in the best way.

She climbed into the shower. After five minutes of hot water, her brain started to think beyond the desire for more sleep or more sex. Why hadn't she looked for the book while he was asleep? Adrian had to have it. He hadn't admitted anything, but he *had* to. He knew the lines, for God's sake. Obviously he'd fucked her brains out. She giggled and then really laughed, her whole body shaking with it in the hot spray of the shower.

Now that she was really awake, she had to admit to herself that she'd probably left the book with him because doing so would mean she'd have to find him privately and ask for it. And that might lead to something delicious. After finding out how good they were together, just getting him out of her system wasn't enough anymore.

She wanted more.

There was no time to go and confront him now. He was probably already at breakfast, and no way was she going to bring up last night or the book in front of her brother or Brad, who was nearly as bad as Adrian and Connor when it came to teasing her. There was so much to do and just no time. She had to meet her brother for breakfast; he'd want to go over their schedule. And there was a writing workshop she wanted to attend before the tourney got started. Her pitch wouldn't take long, but she'd have to step on it to make it to that and then back for the third and fourth rounds of the tourney.

She rushed through her morning routine. Nothing

seemed to be where she expected it to be. First, her hair-brush was missing, and then her skirt for today. She had to look professional to meet the editor. Her hair wouldn't straighten, and her lipstick looked sloppy. She growled at herself and shoved her pitch notes into her purse. In the newbie workshop, they'd said you shouldn't read your pitch from a card, but damn it, she just couldn't seem to remember the *words*.

She hauled open the door. No time to think about her pitch now. There were only minutes to grab a coffee and a pastry from the breakfast buffet. Where had the morning gone? Connor was going to kill her. She huffed as she stood waiting for the elevator. Her cell buzzed with a text from Connor.

You're late

She whipped off a reply. *On my way down*

A is coming up for you, you better be ready

Of course he was. Neither one of them could seem to stop watching out for her. It was getting bloody annoying.

The elevator dinged, and the doors slid open. Adrian and an older couple stood inside. She hesitated and then climbed in. He gave her an odd look. Was he wondering why she'd left in the night? Did it bother him, or was he happy he didn't have to be the one that said, "All right, that was fun, but now back to reality"? Heat spread across her cheeks. How was she going to live through the rest of the weekend?

"You're late." The deep tones of his voice made her want to rewind to last night. Couldn't they just go back and crawl into bed again?

"So Connor tells me." She sniffed. "He send you to take care of me? Again?"

"Again?"

The elevator door opened, and she strode out. A stray lock of hair flipped down into her eyes. Damn it, her bun was coming loose already. What else was going to go wrong?

"Breakfast is already over. They shut the buffet."

She groaned.

He grinned. "But I saved you a few things and a coffee, if Brad didn't scarf it down while I was gone."

"Oh, my God! You're the best. I lo— Ah..." She stumbled, literally and figuratively. Really? After last night, and then leaving him in the dark, she was going to tell him she loved him? What was wrong with her? She couldn't say that, even if it was just a flippant reply to him saving her something to eat. He caught her arm, steadied her. He looked serious, and she suddenly didn't want breakfast, or to hear whatever it was he had to say.

"I'm not hungry. I'll get something later. Tell Connor I'll catch up with him at the tables. I don't need a strategy talk this morning." She pulled away from him and rushed down the hallway, calling over her shoulder, "I need to see the front desk for a minutc."

She was taking off, again. The realization made his breakfast sit in his belly like lead. Last night had been a terrible mistake. Now she couldn't stand to be anywhere near him, not even for a few minutes. What if it was like this from now on? This was exactly why he hadn't wanted to risk their friendship.

He'd woken and realized immediately she was gone. What had he expected? Why would she stay when she knew all too well what he and his family were like? She'd made a pre-emptive strike and left him, first.

And he didn't like it. Not one bit.

He returned to the table where Connor and Brad were talking and laughing, waiting for them.

"Hey, where's Jenn?" Connor frowned at him.

"She had to take care of something at the front desk. And she said she'd catch up with you later."

"What?"

Adrian forced a laugh. "She probably remembers the strategy from the, oh I don't know, million times you talked about it?"

Connor stared at him. Crap. Did he have *I slept with your sister and want to do it again* written all over his face? "It's time to go in. Jenn's already qualified for this round, we all have, but I'm going to watch the latecomers play. See if I can catch any tells."

"Yeah, exactly according to strategy." Connor shook his head but dropped the subject. "Whatever."

They signed for the breakfast bills and walked to the side of the hotel that hosted the tourney. Adrian checked the front reception area but didn't see any sign of Jenn or her delicious little navy suit with its tight skirt and single-breasted blazer. Today she looked like a sharp, sexy businesswoman, one he'd like to see completely undone and bent over the arm of his hotel couch...

"Ah...Earth to Adrian. Wake the hell up, dude."

"What?" He shook his head. Connor was back to staring at him.

"I said, Brad and I are going to take the left side of the room. You take the right. See what you can scout. But if you're this zoned out, I don't think you're going to see much. Didn't you get any sleep last night?"

"Not much." Good God, his voice cracked, for fuck's sake.

"If you can wake up enough, keep your eyes open for

Jenn and get her to watch too. Maybe she'll see what you don't."

Right. No way was Jenn going to show up and hang with him. She'd almost said she loved him this morning, and she sure as hell didn't mean to. Not even in the fun way they'd said it a hundred times as friends. She'd practically bit her own tongue and then dashed away like she was on fire. He'd fucked up their relationship for good, exactly like he knew he would.

He watched the qualifiers for a little more than an hour. But Connor was right, he wasn't learning anything new. He could barely pay attention to the games going on around him. Disgusted, he signed out from the tourney at security and headed for the exit. He texted to Connor he was going for some coffee. On his way to the bar, which doubled as a breakfast area, he looked out into the main reception lobby and spotted the familiar blue dress suit.

Jenn paced from one end of the lobby to the other. Then back again. Her arms were crossed, but she soon dropped them to her sides and gave herself a little shake and then paced the room again. What was the matter with her? She waved her hands, clearly talking to herself. Was she upset over last night or this morning? Why hadn't she come to see the games like her brother had planned?

She paced toward him and then turned to walk away again. He headed over. This was Jenn in a panic, and if it was over him, her anxiety wasn't worth it. He caught up with her at the far corner of the lobby, close to the open double-wide corridor that led to the side of the building where the romance convention was being held.

"Jenn, what's wrong?"

She jumped and swung around to face him. "Nothing. Nothing's wrong. It's just all a little too much. I don't know what I was thinking. How could I believe I could do this? I missed breakfast, missed Connor's strategy, and missed half of *Pitch Perfect*. I'm never going to be ready..."

She rambled on and looked close to tears. Yup, Jenn was in panic mode. He'd seen it before. She just needed a little re-set and she'd be fine, able to take on whatever she needed to. But this wasn't the place for a tickle fight to relax her like he'd done as kids, and he didn't have a car to take her on a joyride like he'd done before her first university exams. Only one thing to do, and his mouth went dry at the image that popped into his head. He might not be around after this weekend, but he could help her now.

Before he could think better of it, he grabbed her, pulled her close, and kissed her.

The pressure of Adrian's lips on hers, the heat from his body as he crushed her against him, and the immediate, intense response that rushed through her brought her thought process, which had been rushing along at a hundred miles per hour, to a grinding halt.

Who cared about the poker tournament or ticking off her brother? He wouldn't stay mad for long over a missed strategy meeting. Who cared if she skipped half the pitching workshop? She wrapped her arms around Adrian and clung. He held her, one arm around her waist and the other across her upper back, his hand cradling the back of her neck. He deepened the kiss and dug his fingers through her hair. The last of her messy bun gave way and she melted. She opened her lips and let his tongue slide inside her, the action immediately bringing to mind the way he'd taken her the night before.

She clutched at his back. It took a moment for her to

recognize the catcalls and cheering coming from behind her. She pulled away, a little gratified by the reluctant way he let go and the lazy, half-shuttered look in his eyes that told her he'd gotten lost in the kiss as well. She glanced behind her and saw Nancy and a few of the other writing friends she'd made at the conference laughing and applauding.

Oh, God. Way to look professional. Heat spread across her cheeks and into her chest until it met her tingling nipples. Not that she would regret the kiss. She took a step back. The writers probably thought this was live performance art for the conference. Adrian was certainly handsome enough.

"What was that for?" She caught the breathless quality in her voice and blushed. By now she probably looked like a tomato.

"Because you looked like you needed it." He hesitated. "And because I wanted to."

And didn't that do things to her.

She smoothed her hands down her skirt and straightened her blazer. The crowd behind her was dispersing, headed to the next workshop, no doubt. That meant it was time for her to go.

"I have a...thing...I have to do."

"All right."

"I'll be back to the tourney after. It won't take long. Five minutes apparently." Her stomach churned at the idea of the future of her book resting on this tiny window of time with her ideal editor. But somehow it didn't seem as bad as before, before Adrian had come after her. He'd saved her again. Would that ever stop? Hopefully not, if saving her meant erotic little encounters like this one.

"All right."

"I'll make it back to the tourney for the next round, no problem."

"All right."

Was that all he could say? He appeared out of nowhere, like a hero from a romance novel, and saved her from herself, and all he could say was "all right"? So much for her interest in the strong silent type. She bit her lip and tried not to laugh at herself. Adrian was a lot more than some hunk in a book, but good grief. She patted him on the arm and walked away.

She fished her notes out of her purse and strode to the pitch session room. She could do this.

The bar buzzed with a hundred voices—women from the conference escaping for a coffee and men from the poker tourney waiting for round three to begin. The two groups kept to themselves, but maybe there was a story there, a romance? Jenn grinned as she headed to the far corner where she could see her brother, Brad, and Adrian's tall silhouettes. She'd better get her next plot laid out soon because she'd done it! She'd nailed her pitch with not only the editor of her dreams, but her second choice, too. Both publishers had requested the full book to read, and she couldn't stop grinning. She worked hard not to skip over to the bar, but hadn't been able to stop the little dance she'd performed after she exited the pitch room. The authors waiting had shared her joy. That was something she hadn't expected about the whole writing thing. The other authors and the way they supported each other.

"Hi!" she chirped at the boys.

"About time you showed up. You missed all the

secondary qualifying rounds. Where have you been?" her brother groused.

"I had some stuff to do. Did I miss much?" She looked at Adrian, but he looked away.

Connor sighed, his long-suffering expression one she was all too familiar with but not one that worried her. "Not really. The better players qualified last night. Are you ready to play today?" Her brother was always quick to give her a hard time, but just as swift to forgive her.

"Oh, yeah. I am going to kick ass today." She grinned at Connor and Brad, who raised his coffee cup to her. Adrian nodded his head, but didn't really meet her eyes. What was with him?

She wanted desperately to tell Adrian about what had happened, about how his kiss had saved her, and the fantastic way she felt right now about writing. She was doing it! She was making this weekend work in all the best ways. She'd accomplished her major goal of speaking to an editor and getting them interested in her book. She was learning what she could from the conference and meeting some fun writers. And she was playing well enough at the table. And last night... Last night she'd finally had the mind blowing sex of her dreams with the man of her dreams.

But she couldn't tell him. Not here with her brother and Brad listening, and not later, really, unless she was ready to admit she wanted to take him back to his bed to properly celebrate her successful pitch. Admitting she wanted him again? Yup. Sure. Admitting the feelings she'd experienced while writing the book? Nope. Not a chance. And the book would come up this time. Last night they'd danced around it, but that wouldn't happen again. She wanted her baby back. Besides, he seemed to be ignoring her.

Was he worried she'd spill the beans and reveal their

one-nighter to her brother? She mulled the possibilities over as Conner blathered on about strategy. She nodded her head at the appropriate moments, and they walked as a group to stand in line in front of the doors to the tourney.

What a buzzkill. Maybe Adrian was freaked out because he couldn't get over the fact that she was his best friend's little sister. Not that he'd seemed bothered by it last night. But maybe last night was the only night she was going to get.

She pressed her lips together. No way. Goal one was done, and she was off to play cards for goal two, but she wanted more of goal three...time alone in bed with Adrian, naked and sweaty. He wasn't out of her system yet. And in all honesty, she didn't want him to be. She just needed to make sure he felt the same.

CHAPTER EIGHT

IT WAS easy to let Connor convince Adrian to come with him and Jenn to see a show. This was Vegas after all, and how could anyone go and not see a show? Plus, he'd done well today, played a decent couple of games and, most importantly, didn't give in to the urge to hang off Jenn.

Brad wasn't coming. He'd made himself pretty scarce, something about not wanting to leave the tournament, which was totally unnecessary. More likely it was something to do with the lady player he'd been hanging around.

But all that really mattered was Jenn. She looked fantastic. She also looked a little annoyed. What was she missing now at her romance conference? She wore a little black dress that clung in all the right places. And she smelled incredible; he hadn't been able to stop himself from leaning in and breathing her in when they'd ridden the elevator down to the lobby. Now, in the back of their limo, it was all he could do to remember her brother sat on her other side.

"This is going to be great. Do you remember that awful

play Jenn was in in high school? The one where she was the alien?" Connor said.

Jenn grinned. "The *lead* alien, thank you very much. And it wasn't awful."

"Oh, yes, it was. But you made a great lead alien." Adrian grinned back at her.

"You drove all the way from your university to come." Jenn had that look in her eyes. The one that said *kiss me*.

Or maybe that's how he always saw her. This was getting out of hand so quickly. Making love to her last night only made him want her more tonight. And her damn dress, caught by the seat's leather, was inching up.. An image, bright with detail, slid into his mind of running his hand up her thighs, stroking her pussy until she opened her legs wide for him.

Jesus, he was going straight to hell. Maybe he was there already.

Connor was looking at him. Did he say something? Connor's cell phone rang, and he was spared from asking and coming across like an idiot.

"Hello? Hey, slow down. Okay, right. I'll be back in twenty minutes." Connor looked serious. "Brad had an issue with hotel security. I'm going back after we drop you two off."

"What? But you'll miss the play." Jenn put a hand on her brother's arm. "Do you want us to go back with you?"

"No, you guys go and have fun. I'll clear things up for Brad. He's lost all his ID." He grimaced and shook his head. "I don't know the details, but he needs someone to vouch for him."

Adrian pressed his lips together. Oh, so not good. He was going to be left alone with Jenn at the play. Jenn, who looked like the perfect date, who *was* his perfect date.

Jenn laughed easily at the round of jokes. A comedy musical. Connor didn't know what he was missing. The cast was kicking, and once they got seated with a drink, Adrian was the perfect date—attentive, amusing, and gorgeous, just as always.

It was impossible to forget what being with him in bed had been like. Desire slid through her, harder than it had when she was younger and crushing on him. Hotter than when she'd seen him last and understood the crush had never gone away. She'd always loved him, and now, having had a nibble, she wanted to savor the man, keep him here beside her, enjoy him in and out of bed for as long as she could. Forever? Not a word she imagined before when she thought of love for herself, but it was there, on the tip of her tongue.

Intercession came, and everyone rushed from their seats. She had no desire to leave their table and join the crazy lineup for another drink. Both she and Adrian had nursed theirs, and she still had most of her drink left.

"I love this."

He looked startled. "What?"

"This—the play, the night, being with you."

"Jenn—"

"No, really. You haven't been around much this last year. The play is great, but it's great to see you. And what you did this morning"—she rushed on since it looked like he was going to reject her happiness, and she couldn't have that, not now—"you saved me. That kiss... I was losing it, as I am sure you were aware. I got through my pitch today because of you."

He relaxed, clearly all right with the idea of helping her, but not of her loving him. Well, too bad.

"And last night. I can't imagine anything better than last night. Except what tonight will be like." She gave him her very best, most wicked smile.

His jaw might fall off if it kept gaping like that but, damn, it felt good to be bad around him. She kept her eyes on his while she took a drink so she didn't miss it—the flash of heat in his eyes. He definitely wanted her.

"I fully expect you to take me to bed tonight, Adrian Cooper. And I expect it to be damn good."

His jaw clicked shut, and a muscle quivered in his cheek. Then he leaned forward and laid gentle lips on hers. They only stayed gentle for a minute. Then he took the kiss deeper until her head was spinning. When they came up for air, he had a satisfied look on his face, and it was her that was shocked at the response screaming from her body.

He grinned. "Since this is Vegas, I'll ante up." He sobered then, and she shivered. "Just remember, Jenn, there's always an end to the game."

The lights dimmed, and Jenn sat back with a huff. Did he mean that he was only playing along because, 'What happens in Vegas stays in Vegas'? Or that someone was, as in any game, going to be the loser? That would be her. Well, she'd pay the price. For another night of memories that wouldn't stay in Vegas but come home with her. How could she not?

At the hotel, she had a moment of nerves. Could she really handle another night with him, knowing he probably didn't want more? But he held her hand, gently, and they made their way to her room together. She expected another night of wild sex, expected they'd begin as hot as they had the previous night, all flash fire and explosions, but he surprised her.

"I love this dress." He ran his hands over the black material, stroking her through the fabric. He leaned in to kiss her jaw. She stilled, then arched her neck when he kissed her throat. What was he doing, playing it soft and sweet if this was the only night they had left? She would have protested, but he cupped her breast, and her words were lost as his lips met hers.

He was gentle, took his time, and made her nearly weep with the slow way he undressed her. And when she was naked, he stared at her for a moment before he swept her off her feet and took her to the bed.

If she'd thought she'd wanted him as much as possible before, she was wrong. Now she ached for him.

This would be their last night. It had to be. So he was going to make it everything he couldn't be for her later. When he stroked her, she responded, reaching out for him. The feel of her skin, the scent of her, the way her eyes had glazed with pleasure, made him wild, but he kept control of his desire with an iron fist and tasted her, every inch of her, with a delight that eventually broke him and had him thrusting inside her.

Even then he waited, took it slowly, made her peak twice just to hear the tremble in her voice as she called his name.

Something he would never forget.

And when she slept after he'd pleasured her the second time, he slipped from the room and went back to his own.

"Damnit." He slammed his hand down on the desk in his room. Even now, after deciding that was it, that their second night together was all he could give without tearing them both up inside. He wanted to go back. Wanted to be with her again. Not even to have sex, just to hold her. But that would end up hurting her more, give her hope where she shouldn't have any.

He'd probably already smashed the friendship that had grown between them for years, and maybe even damaged the one he had with her brother.

He was worse than an idiot.

He couldn't love her. It was impossible. A tiny voice inside reminded him of his brother. His brother loved his wife, but it had still gone wrong. He shook his head and headed for the shower. If he didn't wash off her alluring scent , right now, he was going to break all his rules and go back to her, beg her to let him in.

And there was no one but him to blame for the heartbreak that was sure to come because he couldn't control his own desire.

CHAPTER NINE

THE TOURNEY ROOM rang with a hushed roar of sound —the players and dealers talking, the TV crew filming with their machines whirring, the security and staff and the few live spectators milling in the background, the shuffle, flick, and tap of cards and chips against each other and the felted tables. But he could hear one sound above everything else, and it was driving him crazy—Jenn's laughter.

She sat at the table directly behind him, playing with three other women entered in the women's competition. She had to be doing well, kicking ass, just like she'd claimed she would. Something sure had her pumped up. He saw that the moment she'd joined them in the bar. Whatever she'd been worried about earlier must have passed, because this was Jenn on a roll. And Jenn on a roll usually meant trouble.

She laughed again, and his balls tightened. She'd sounded a lot like that last night, only huskier, when she'd ridden him like a cowgirl. He couldn't risk a glance back at her. He had to keep his eyes on the game, and he couldn't let her see him looking and think there was something more he could offer her than last night's fun and games.

Of course, there *was* another night left.

"Sir, you have the bet," the dealer said.

Attention on the table. Adrian checked his cards and slid some chips to the center, doubling the pool. Seven-card stud again, same as when he'd played with Jenn against the dealer at the learners' table. Fourth street brought him nothing, but fifth gave him a near perfect straight. Sixth made it perfect.

"Call." Another player called the game at the seventh straight, but no one could beat Adrian's hand. After the dealer announced him as the winner, he smiled and stood, rolled his shoulders, and stretched his neck. He walked to the edge of the room and checked the digital score boards. He'd qualified for the fourth round, although it was by the skin of his teeth. Now the games would get longer, and harder. Connor was set for the next round, but Brad was even lower on the boards than Adrian. If he didn't pick up speed, he'd be out.

Jenn giggled. He turned, and she was right beside him, staring up at the board. She'd qualified as well, no surprise there. She really was good at poker. And writing. And kissing and sex...

She looked at him with one eyebrow raised, a naughty glint in her eye like she knew exactly what he'd been thinking. "Want to go upstairs and have a quick celebration before dinner?"

Oh, God. How to say no to a proposition like that? But if he gave in, he might not ever stop giving in, until one day, giving in meant leaving. He couldn't do that to her. He gave her a smile and hoped it wasn't as pained as he felt. "Sorry.

I've got to get a little rest. I'll meet you back for dinner with the guys."

He didn't miss the hurt in her eyes. It punched him, right in the gut. This was exactly what he had wanted to avoid, and a repeat of last night would make the next "no" so much harder. He turned and walked away. Better to do this quick, now, so no hearts ended up broken.

His already felt bruised, battered.

Well, didn't that suck. She hadn't imagined he was giving her the cold treatment. And this was more than that; it was a direct brush off. Her cheeks burned. He'd said no and then walked away from her like he hadn't just insulted her.

"Hey, good playing, sis." Connor bumped shoulders with her, his relaxed and friendly touch a balm to her dignity.

"You too. Nice to see you near the top." Had Adrian seen her brother coming up behind them and cut things short to avoid embarrassing her? Maybe. But that didn't seem like his reason to reject her.

"We're holding our own. Brad's got his mind on other things though. He might not make it long in the tourney." Connor nodded to the corner of the room where Jenn could see Brad talking to a slender woman. "Can't blame him."

Jenn rubbed the back of her neck. "Hmm." They all seemed to have had their reasons to come to Vegas, and not all of them were for poker. "I think I'm going up to my room to grab some Advil. Too much coffee this morning. I'll catch you in a bit." Her head really was aching. The lack of sleep was catching up, along with this morning's highs and lows.

She made her way through the press of people exiting

the tourney room, swiftly changing direction when she saw the camera crew trying to catch a few players for short interviews. She wasn't in the mood to deal with that. She slipped out the other exit doors and back into the hallway that led to the coat check. From her earlier little games of hide and seek with Adrian, she knew there was a set of back corridors that would bring her around to the far entrance of the main foyer, and then she could back-track to the elevators, avoiding the poker reality show.

She left the crowds behind after the first corner, and no one was using the coat check. The bored attendant had retreated to playing games on her iPhone. Jenn walked past and headed to the back hallway. Unfortunately her escape route was completely blocked. The hall was stacked with chairs, and hotel staff rushed back and forth, obviously setting up a room for some sort of banquet. She rubbed her temple, sighed, and turned to head back the way she'd come.

The sound of Adrian's voice stopped her short. Now was so not the time to talk to him again. She'd used up her allotment of bravery for the day, riding on the wave of excitement over her pitch and her game and asking him to bed to celebrate. She hesitated. He sounded like he was talking to someone. She took a quick glance around the corner and ducked back, grateful he'd had his back to her. This weekend was beginning to feel like she was playing a game of cat and mouse. He was talking on his cell, and considering the stiff way he was holding himself, he didn't seem too happy about it.

She pressed against the corner wall. As long as he didn't come back here, she was safe. The staff were all busy and probably wouldn't care that she looked like an idiot, eavesdropping on the guy she'd slept with last night. She strained to hear what he was saying.

"Look, Mom… Exactly what is happening there?"

His voice started to fade. This was terrible. He was talking to his *mother*, for heaven's sake. One of the waiters shuffling chairs gave her a look. Great. Now she was a spy, or a peeping Tom, or something. She was going to end up getting black-balled from the hotel. She poked her head around the corner again, just in time to see him start to turn toward her. She ducked back in again, and her body flushed —hot then cold. If he caught her, she'd never hear the end of it.

"Jared moved back in with you? As in, permanently? I thought he was just staying with you for a while?"

Jenn frowned and bit her lip. This sounded serious. Her stomach clenched. Adrian didn't deserve to have her listen in on his family problems. She looked back at the blocked hallway and sighed. But she wasn't going anywhere. She could stand here with her fingers in her ears, but that would look even worse if Adrian did come around the corner and spot her. Aside from last night, he still seemed to think she wasn't capable of taking care of herself. Looking like she was eight again wouldn't help things.

"I thought Jared and Emma were going to try and sort things out… Wow. He actually caught her in bed with some-one? Do you need me to come home?"

And there it was. Adrian to the rescue again. He was always fixing things for someone. It made him the best kind of friend, of course, someone who you could always count on. It was hard to stay mad at him. He had helped her yesterday morning, too, with that kiss. It was a strange thing to do if he wanted to her to forget all about them getting together, but the distraction of his lips on hers had really helped her push through her nerves and go for her pitch on a high. But was he going to leave now and ruin her last chance at being with him and getting him out of her nighttime fantasies? If he wouldn't stay with her because of her brother, or their past, or whatever, she had to make sure she could move on. Two nights hadn't done it.

His voice faded again. She couldn't hear what he was saying. When she looked, he was on the move, walking away from her. Why had he slept with her, knowing as he must—having read her book or at least part of it—that she wanted him for more than a fling and hoped they could be together?

The thoughts buzzed in her aching head. Adrian was gone now, and she was free to head to her room for some much-needed pain killers. In a minute. She leaned against the wall and tilted her head back against the cool surface. She was all too aware of what she wanted from Adrian. But what did he want from her?

This was *so* getting old. Jenn rushed to her room to drop off her notebook and the fabulous handouts she'd gotten at the morning workshop. Mornings at the writing workshops, lunches with her brother, games in the afternoon, sneaking off to the writing social stuff in the evening, and then back to the poker table—the whirlwind action was exhausting, and she was starting to feel like she was losing traction. According to Nancy, it could be months before she heard back from either editor she wasn't getting the full benefit of the writing workshops, and her heart wasn't in the poker. Worst of all, there'd been no action at all when it came to goal number three since their naughty poker game. There was only today, tonight, and tomorrow morning and then they would all be going home.

The bed looked so tempting. She could just curl up in it and forego the rest of everything. Or slip on the bathing suit she'd brought with the insane idea of going for a dip in the pool. When did she think she would have the time when she'd packed that? She walked to the washroom and ran her hands under the tap. She glanced in the mirror. She looked good, but maybe a little tired. Time for a pep talk.

"Okay, Jenn. Get a grip. You are not giving up quite yet. You have made huge progress with the writing. Adrian is probably going to be a wash, but someday, when you feel better, he'll be a hell of a fun Vegas memory." She grinned at herself. Damn straight he would. The sex had been everything she'd imagined and more.

The smile faded. Too bad that was all it was. She had to admit, based on her disappointment, that the reality of their short affair not becoming more that that was fairly harsh. She'd wanted a lot more.

They'd been good friends for a long time. He'd always been there for her, a comfort in a way her brother couldn't be—an outsider but still close enough to listen to her worries and be counted on for an honest opinion and real support. He gave the best hugs, and if they meant more to her than they had for him, well, that was the real heartbreaker.

She dried her hands and touched up her hair. Time to go face the Southern belle wanna-be poker princess and wipe her off the scoreboard. She might not make it much farther in the tourney—none of the team but Connor probably would—but she could beat that woman and make her brother happy he invited her. This trip would not be a total wreck.

She stepped outside the door and nearly bumped into her brother. He grabbed her in a quick hug.

"Hey, you. You ready?"

Connor let her go, and she gave him a smile. Adrian lurked behind him, but she avoided looking at him. Really, as soon as she finished in the tournament, she was out of here. She'd tell her brother the truth and enjoy the last of the writing conference tonight when they gave out the awards to the best romance writers of the year. To heck with poker or men. Considering her performance at the game and his success, Connor would be cool with that. If he won this next round, he might even forget for a while about teasing her about writing romance. That would be good since she was going to ask for her book back from Adrian, and the truth would come out. Then she was going to write murder mystery for a while. She knew just who her first victim would be—one tall hunk of man named Adrian. Purely fictional, of course.

"Yeah, let's do this."

▭

They headed as a group to the elevator, but he might as well have been on his own. Connor was wrapped up in the game, Brad had his mind on the woman he'd met, and Jenn, well, she seemed to be done with him. It was probably for the best, and a direct result of his behavior, but that didn't mean he had to like it. His phone vibrated in his pocket. He clenched his teeth. He was not taking another call from home or another round of fifty texts from his brother ranging from anger to hurt to desperation to get his wife back.

At least for once it hadn't been one of his family

dumping their wife. He wasn't about to get further involved though, not right now. Even though the offer to his mom had been honest—he would go home if she needed him—he really didn't want to step into a personal tangle that sounded like the plot of a romance novel. He had enough of that right here. He had promised Connor he'd do his best with the poker, and he had to clear the air with Jenn. The list of what he had to do in the next twenty-four-hour period was pretty long, and he had to admit, if only to himself, he wished it included another night with Jenn in his bed.

Sleeping with her had been a mistake, although he couldn't quite bring himself to regret their time together. She didn't deserve to be hurt though. He had to apologize for taking their relationship out of the friend zone. Unfortunately, that apology would have to include the real fact he wasn't going to be there for her and why. And he had to give back her book. That was going to be fun. She'd probably kill him. But at least her being angry was better than being hurt.

The four of them split up as they passed through security and walked to their next assigned table. There were fewer players now, and more spectators as the better players had moved up the scoreboard and the rookie players stayed on to watch. This could be a long afternoon, or a very short one, depending on how the cards played out.

⬚

Adrian stood and nodded to the other players. "Good game."

"See you next year, Cooper."

"Maybe." Or maybe not. Right now he'd had enough of Vegas, and he really hadn't seen much outside of the hotel. No way was he coming back here where memories of his time with Jenn would plague him. He looked around as he stepped away from the table. He was done; having lost this last hand he was out of the tourney. Brad was out too—he'd only lasted two hands in this round and had left for the bar more than an hour ago.

Connor was still in and had qualified for the big hands. He'd done really well. But then he didn't have a woman distracting him like Brad, or Adrian. He stretched and ran his hand through his hair. There were only a dozen tables in use now, and most of the spectators were crowded around three tables in particular. He checked the scoreboard. The women's competition was finished, and Jenn had done well, coming in third. That meant she'd take home a small part of that kitty but not move into the final rounds of the overall tournament. He looked for her slender form and dark hair. Where was she? It seemed like he'd spent the last few days wondering that very question.

He left the game room and headed for the bar. A quick look there revealed no Jenn. She could be in her room, but it was more likely she'd gone to spend some time at the writer's conference. She had to be exhausted, running back and forth between the two events. Not to mention the fact that neither one of them had much sleep the last couple of nights.

He was tired. And he had a persistent ache in his chest at the thought she might not want to see him if he did find her. He headed for the elevators. Now was a good time to go back to his room and get a little rest. And maybe to finish reading her book. He only had the end to read now, and finishing it felt important, something he had to do, before he gave the pages back to her.

The ride seemed to take too long. He leaned against the elevator wall. Jenn had looked so good that first day when they had ridden in the elevator together. He hadn't seen her in a while, and seeing her made him remember all the years of them growing up together. She was beautiful, a far cry from when he'd pulled her half-drowned from the family pool. Definitely all grown up and everything he liked in a woman. And last night... He shifted his weight. God, he wanted her again. Too bad he wasn't good enough for her. This latest breakup with his brother aside, the men in his family just weren't reliable.

The elevator signaled his floor, and he walked toward his room. He hesitated when he spotted Jenn standing near his door. Her dark brown hair hung in loose waves he could lose himself in, and her dress clung to her. He could live without that, looking at her, touching her, though it was going to be hard. But her eyes—they pulled at him, gorgeous, sad, hungry. A look he knew too well.

"Why did you take it?"

The book. That's all she wanted. Not more of him. "Come in." He keyed the door open. How was he going to explain this? He walked inside and she followed silently. The words tumbled out. "It was an accident. When I went to get my key from Connor's room, your door was open. I sort of...found myself inside. It was on your bed, and I sat down for a minute... And then I accidently knocked it over. I grabbed the pages and realized what you were doing and what you were writing."

She didn't respond. She watched him and the look in her eyes hadn't changed.

"It was us. And it was so hot, so sexy. It blew my mind. It was good too, really well written."

She straightened at that, like he'd said something wrong. He took a step toward her. "I had to read it all."

"Did you finish it? Or did you just read the sex?" Her

lips pressed into a firm line. She was pissed, that was clear enough, and he couldn't blame her.

"I read it all except the ending. I came up now to finish. I was going to give it back. I just need to know how it ends." He reached for her, but she took a step back.

"I think we know that, don't we? How dare you think you have to break into my room to check up on me. I don't need that. I don't need someone to take care of me."

"Yes, you do. You always have. But I can't be that for you. I can't be there, won't be there. The men in my family, they don't do commitment, they don't have it in them to care for a woman properly. You know that. My grandfather, my father, and now my brother. None of us can give forever. And you deserve better."

"But it was okay to take my work and read it like a smut rag? Did it get you so horny you just couldn't help yourself? You had to sleep with me to get it out of your system? Well, I have news for you. I came here partially to get *you* out of *my* system. I guess you could say I've done that. I am a grown woman, Adrian Cooper. No one wants or needs to be watched over forever. I know how to take care of myself, and I know what I want and what I need." Her voice cracked and so did his heart.

"Jenn—"

"Maybe you should read this." She dropped the sheaf of papers on the table and started for the door.

He wouldn't stop her; this had to happen. She had to be safe from what would take place if they tried to make it work.

She turned back to him before she opened the door. "Read it and figure out we could have had something. I have some news for you. You're always taking care of someone. Me, Connor, your friends, your brother and mother. You aren't your father or your grandfather, or you wouldn't be the friend you are. And I heard you say your brother wants his wife back. He's not afraid of commitment. But since you can't see that and are so sure you have to live alone, go ahead. I don't need you."

She stormed out. He let her go, stunned. What she had said was true.

But was it all true?

CHAPTER TEN

"OH, come on. We have to celebrate!" Connor wheedled through their joined door. "We need to go to dinner and toast our success!"

Some success. She had accomplished two out of three goals, pitching her book and placing high enough in the poker tournament to make some cash. But goal number three was a complete disaster and clearly had left her off worse for wear than when she'd started this crazy plan. "I'm too tired, Connor. Go away." She flopped backward onto her bed and stared at the ceiling.

"You can't be that tired. You've been up here for hours! And you placed third in the women's branch! And hello, I made it to fifth overall! We kicked ass."

"Not all of us."

"Adrian held his own and Brad, well, he's been distracted. But our team placed in the top quarter. It's our last night here. Come on."

"No."

"I'll buy."

He wasn't going to leave her alone. He'd bug her until she gave in and went with them. She really was tired, but it wasn't really her body that ached with exhaustion. It was her heart. She looked at her watch. If she went with them, she could leave right after and go see the awards ceremony. That would distract her for a little while from the memory of the look in Adrian's eyes when she'd confronted him in his room. She should have thrown the bloody book at him.

"Fine. Let me get changed."

Connor laughed. "You have fifteen minutes until our reservation."

Great. She ticked off the list in her head. Fifteen minutes, an hour for dinner, and an evening with the writers. Then she'd come to her room and pack because she was changing her plane reservations to leave first thing in the morning.

The steak tasted like cardboard. And the potatoes like... okay, potatoes. But she wasn't enjoying any of it, not while Adrian stared at her and tried to cajole her into talking about the poker game. She didn't want to talk about it. Or rather, she didn't want to talk to him. Did he think she could just go back to being friends? Well, maybe she could, but not for a while. They'd been friends forever. But it was going to take a while to get the sting out. Connor and Brad didn't seem to notice the by-play, their discussion revolving around Connor's last hands, the upcoming tournament in Atlantic City, and next year's tournament here.

If they asked her to come with them, she'd vomit.

There was only her drink to get through, and then she'd plead exhaustion whether Connor liked it or not. She'd go and watch the awesome writers she loved talk about romance, why they loved it, and why they wrote it. Maybe that would remind her why it had been worth trying something with Adrian.

He was looking at her. She looked back, stared right in his eyes. He was the first to look away. Why had she spoiled a perfectly good fantasy with this man? She'd already changed the name of her hero in her book. And her heroine. The names meant nothing now.

Do something. *Do something!* Jenn was leaving again, and all he could seem to do was sit there and watch. She was probably headed to the writing convention again, but something inside him told him it might be a long time until he saw her again after this.

"You're seriously going back to your room? Come on, Jenn, it's Las Vegas! You can't spend your last night in your room. We're going over to some of the casinos. Come party with us!" Connor urged, but it was easy to see she'd made her mind up.

"I'm tired."

"You've been tired all weekend. What's wrong?" Connor half stood in his seat. He wasn't letting this go, and really, Adrian couldn't blame him. It was an easy observation to make—Jenn had had her mind on something else all weekend.

She held up a hand and shook her head. "Not right now, okay?" She stood. "I'll see you in the morning. I'm flying out early, but I'll catch you at breakfast."

Connor turned to him. "What the hell have you done?"

"Me?" Oh God, if Connor found out that he'd slept with his sister... He exchanged quick, alarmed glances with

Jenn. From the look on her face, she clearly didn't want her brother to know either, and as illogical as it was, didn't that smart a bit.

"Yes, you. You were with her last. She has to be mad at you. Did you mess up another one of her crazy plans? Tell me I am not going to have to deal with some sort of fallout when I get home."

He didn't know they'd slept together. That was a relief, but a short-lived one. She was leaving and was going to forget all about what they'd shared. Could he really let that happen? Was she right, could they have had something? Her book certainly had a happy ending.

"Hello, I am right here. He didn't mess up anything." Jenn crossed her arms.

"Well what is going on? I know you, and something is definitely wrong."

What could he say that wouldn't tell her brother they'd had an affair or that she'd been sneaking off to the writing conference? "Look, Connor—"

"I was going to tell you about this later, much later, but I might as well tell you now." Jenn didn't look too happy.

He sucked in a breath. What was she going to tell her brother? Would she admit that they'd been together? What would that mean?

"I am a writer. I write romance. Hot, sexy love stories. Trashy novels, as I am sure you will be quick to point out." She put her hands on her hips, and her eyes narrowed. "And I really, really like doing it. When you asked me to come this weekend and I found out the local branch of the Romance Writers' Association was meeting in this very hotel, I figured it was fate."

"What?" Connor's jaw seemed to be a little loose.

"I've been sneaking over to attend the conference."

"She's really good, Connor," Adrian added. She was, too. Her book made him think of all sorts of possibilities he'd long ago put aside.

"You know about this?" Connor stood too. Brad was the only one still seated, and his blond head swiveled back and forth like he was watching a three-way tennis match.

"Yeah, I found out when I got worried that something was up and got too snoopy for my own good."

"I am good, or at least I'm going to be." Jenn sounded defiant. "I have a lot to learn. Thus, the conference. And because I didn't want to be bugged by my brother, his buddy, or *Mister I-Know-What's-Best-For-Everyone* here, I had to do a lot of crazy, exhausting sneaking around."

They were attracting a bit of a crowd, and Adrian was sure he saw someone taking notes. Goddamn crazy writers. Just what he needed—to be the focus of another romance book.

"But I don't need anyone watching over me. I am just fine on my own."

He was right before—she was beautiful when she was pissed off. And she was right. She didn't need a caretaker. She'd been just fine when she was in college. He hadn't been around then since he'd been working several states away and hadn't seen her for months at a time. Neither had her brother. And she'd survived just fine. Bloomed really, given the confidence she had now. She'd changed a lot in those four years, and he had seen it the last few times he'd been home. She was sure of herself, and she'd obviously found her passion in writing.

Maybe he'd been taking care of his family for too long. Maybe, like her, they would do better on their own with a little space and without his constant watching. Jenn was right—he wasn't his father. He'd gone the opposite direction and, instead of running away, had taken control and maybe held on too tight.

"Now you can save your jokes and crap for later. I am not sneaking around anymore. I really appreciate you bringing me here, Connor. It's an opportunity I wouldn't have been able to afford. But much as I loved the poker games, I'm going now to get changed, and tonight I'm watching the awards ceremony. Tomorrow I'm going home. You can joke all you want then."

Shit. She was leaving. This couldn't be happening. He couldn't let it happen.

He watched her turn and walk away, tracking her steps all the way to the door to the bar. And then he stared at the door for a while. The sound of a clearing throat had him turning toward her brother.

"Well? What the hell are you waiting for?" Connor and Brad stared at him.

"What do you mean?"

Connor gave him a look of disbelief. "Do you think I don't know how romance books go? Or that you've been seeing her this weekend? This is where you go after her, stupid."

Jenn shifted in her seat and thanked another of Nancy's friends for their compliment on the dress she'd carefully selected at home for her first ever romance writer's awards night. From the pictures she'd seen online, people tended to go fancy to these events. She hadn't gone overboard with the royal blue lace dress. After all, she was only a newbie, not a nominee. But someday, maybe. Tonight, she'd enjoy herself if it killed her and watch some of her favorite and perhaps new favorite authors receive some well-deserved recognition.

But the inside of the bodice was itchy.

And the dinner she'd consumed with her brother and his buddies sat in her belly like a rock. There was a dinner provided with the ceremony, but she'd had to eat something with Connor or he'd have known something was up. And then she'd blabbed it all out anyway. A drink was definitely in order.

"I'm going to get a drink from the bar. Do you want anything?" she asked Nancy, who, as it turned out, was waiting for her turn on the podium to present an award.

"They're coming around with bottles of wine for the tables now if that helps. Bad day?"

"I guess you could say that. I told my brother that I'm a writer and what I write."

"Ouch. Having a family that doesn't support you can be the worst," Nancy said, and the other ladies agreed in a chorus.

"Well, he's usually pretty good. I mean, he'll make fun, but he'll come around. He's a good guy."

"So what's the real problem? The guy that gave you that hot kiss in the hotel front entrance?" All the women at the table leaned forward to listen.

Jenn pressed her lips together. How could someone whom she'd only met a couple of days ago be so perceptive? "Maybe."

"Did he react badly to the writing?"

"No, he thought it was good." At least he'd said so. And he'd seemed to be sincere. It was easy to picture him in his room when he told her he wanted to read the end. If only he wasn't a complete idiot about everything else.

"So what's the issue?" Nancy's sincere gaze pinned her.

"I don't know. I wanted more, I guess, than a Vegas affair."

"Well, you'd better figure out what you really wanted because he's coming your way, right now."

Jenn's mouth dried as she turned in the direction Nancy was gazing. He looked good in dress pants and jacket with an opened, collared shirt. Apparently lots of others thought so too, from the murmurs around the table. Somehow, he'd appropriated a serving towel and a bottle of the convention labeled wine and was headed straight for their table.

"Hello, story fodder coming up," one of the writers beside her quipped.

"The cover model who wasn't a cover model. Sounds like a rom-com to me," another said, and Jenn looked at her. No way was her life turning into a romantic comedy.

"Ladies. Who wants a glass of white?" Adrian asked, then bent in from her left to serve the woman beside her.

His voice sent a shiver down her back. She was never going to get him out of her system. "What are you doing here?" she whispered at him.

"Bringing a peace offering?" He reached across her and collected her glass to fill it with wine.

"Can I pour it over your head?"

"Jenn," Nancy interjected, "they're about to open the ceremony."

"Fine." Jenn stood and stalked away from the table. Behind her, she heard Adrian make a quick apology. What could he want now? She walked faster toward the door, but he caught up with her anyway and caught her by the elbow.

She stopped. "What do you want?" She looked up at him. He looked so good, so sexy and serious, and he smelled like everything she ever wanted rolled up in one fantasy she couldn't have. Why was he dragging this out longer? He'd already made it perfectly clear that what happened in Vegas stayed there.

"This isn't the best place to do this, but...I made a mistake."

Tears threatened. Jenn pressed her lips together. No way was she losing it, not in front of him or in front of a hundred writers all looking for their next story.

"Yes, you did. So don't make another one here. You said it yourself. You can't do commitment."

"I was wrong about that. About all of it. I've wanted you since you were sixteen. I think I loved you for that long, too."

"Oooh," a lady called out. "Look, Julie, it's performance art! Don't they look just like the cover of Nora's latest book?"

They were gathering an audience. This was crazy. And he'd just told her he loved her?

"I'm getting out of here. It's too late. This was one of my goals, to see where we could go, but it's too late." Jenn tried to brush past him and their gaggle of onlookers.

She might have made it if he didn't catch her arm again, turn her around into his arms, and give her a deep kiss. A kiss like the one they'd shared days ago, but it was more, this one flavored with an emotion that she couldn't define and that both heated her up and scared her to her toes. Maybe he really could commit.

She took a breath to tell him off, but the air gasped out as quickly as it went in when he picked her up and dropped her into a fireman's hold over his shoulder.

JENN SWATTED his ass like she was playing handball, but he wasn't about to put her down. "This is not professional, you jackass!"

He stayed silent, but since she couldn't see him, he grinned at the people waiting for the elevator beside him. The couple grinned back. Jenn was mad, but not too mad or she'd be using a lot worse curses; professionalism in front of her fellow writers be damned.

"I am going to kill you. I am missing the beginning of the award ceremony!"

Adrian had every intention of making her miss the whole thing.

He strode down the hallway and struggled with the lock on his door, but he didn't put her down until they were safely inside and then he flopped her down on the bed.

Where she bounced right up again like a super bouncy-ball.

"What do you think you are doing? You can't just drag me out of a huge ballroom full of people like a cave man."

"I need you to listen to me. Please."

"I don't need to do anything. You made it perfectly clear—"

He kissed her. Long and deep, until he almost forgot what he was going to say. "I finished reading your book."

"What?" She looked dazed, and it was gratifying to see the blush on her cheeks.

He knew this woman, knew her and loved her. "I read the ending. And it's everything I ever wanted, Jenn. Everything I secretly dreamed all the years when I was sure I couldn't offer anything serious to you, so I wouldn't let myself think of you at all. You laid it all out, ink on paper, in words that were exactly what I feel.

"I'm sorry for being an ass. I'm sorry for pushing you away when I could have held you closer, so much sooner."

She turned away slightly, looking at the sheaf of her papers on the small table beside his bed. "I don't know." She looked back at him. "I need a lover, not a babysitter."

"I love you. I can't lose you. You are creative, sexy, and fun. You've completely ruined me for every other woman out there. I don't want to babysit you...although I do want to be there for you." He pulled the box from his pocket, opened it, and held it out to her. "I want to marry you. Please say yes."

The shock in her eyes said this might be too fast. But the minute he'd realized he loved her, this was the only thing that felt right. Thank God. the lower level of the hotel had a sweet line of gift shops that included a jeweler.

"Yes," she breathed the word. "I love you too."

"I know. All was revealed on page one-forty-seven." He grinned at her as his heart swelled inside him. "But the ending was the clincher. It's going to be a bestseller."

She threw herself at him, and he pulled her down with

him to the bed as her lips met his. The thought of her as his wife wasn't the least frightening, although, knowing Jenn's unerring magnetism for trouble, it probably should be.

The ring box dropped to the bed beside them, and he forgot about it while he ran his hands over the length of her.

"Say it again," she moaned against him and rolled over with him so she could straddle him.

He slid his hands up her back and found the zipper to her dress. "I love you."

"Mmmm. That's good. But I meant the other thing."

It took him a minute because she was grinding against him, the heat of her core pressed against the rapidly growing bulge in his pants. "Bestseller."

"There we go. Now, lover, let's do some research."

He pulled the zipper down and exposed her breasts. Beautiful. He palmed them, they weren't huge or small, but seemed perfect, and the hardness of her nipples told him how much she enjoyed being here with him, feeling him touch her this way.

"Let me get out of this rig." She slipped off him and stood beside the bed while she kicked off her shoes and pulled off her dress. Her underwear was nothing but a blue bit of lace.

"Just a minute." There was one thing he needed to see. Her, naked and willing, and with the ring on her finger. He found the box on the bed and pulled out the ring. "I want to see it on you."

She smiled, and the ache in his chest, the one that might have been there since his father left, eased away. She leaned down to kiss him.

How could her three weekend goals have led to this? A ring on her finger? God, she needed to lead goal-setting work-shops. Or write another book. Now that she knew what a real happy ending felt like, her next romance would be even better. A bestseller, like the man said.

He welcomed her into his arms, and his embrace made her heart pound. She'd dreamed of him, fantasized about being together with him, but that fantasy had never extended so far that she could see herself marrying him. This was so much better.

She held out her hand, and he slipped the ring on her finger. It was beautiful. So was he. And as nice as the stone was on her finger, she wanted him so much more. She kissed his lips and then his jaw, and worked her way down his neck. She took her time unbuttoning his shirt, until her impatience got the best of her . She grabbed the edges, pulled the last three buttons apart, and one went flying across the room. The sound of his laughter made her laugh too.

They struggled together to remove his shoes, socks, and pants. Their underwear almost seemed to dissolve in the heat between them. God, the feel of his skin against hers made her shiver in delight. She kissed him, and long minutes slid by as they tasted and explored, slower than they had before. Finally, he pinned her under him and settled between her legs.

The look in his eyes was serious. She'd seen it before, when he helped her escape one trouble or another. But this time she knew what it was, what it meant. He thrust slowly into her, taking his time, filling her inch by inch. She let him have his way—there'd be time enough later for her to have hers. He wanted to care for her because he loved her. That was always going to be a part of him. It wasn't a bad thing, now that he understood she could return the favor.

He stroked her clit gently, insistently, pulling her thoughts away and replacing them with pleasure, until she cried out with the intensity of it.

This was goal number three. She hadn't wanted to admit to herself that he was goal number one, that he meant more to her than a fling or getting him out of her system. Adrian D. Cooper, in the flesh, and he was all hers.

JENN KISSED his shoulder and snuggled deeper against Adrian. This was how life was meant to be—spent from a bout of passion, held by the man she'd wanted forever. He kissed the top of her head, and she looked up into his satisfied expression. She could still hardly believe they'd gotten married. Or that so much else had changed. Her book had been picked up and pushed through the publisher's system to fill a gap in their schedule. Things didn't normally go this fast for new authors, but she was enjoying the ride.

The phone rang, and she considered not answering. But only a few people knew where they'd gone to settle in after her very first book signing tour; a sweet bed and breakfast place that has so far served them well for both a refuge from the busy day with the tour and a place to celebrate their honeymoon. With a sigh, she picked up the phone and clicked talk.

"Hello?"

"Why are you answering the phone?"

Jenn grinned. "Why are you calling me?"

Her brother snorted. "Who says I'm calling you? I'm looking for the big guy. There's a game coming up, and now that he's not totally distracted by some little chickie, I expect my best player back."

"Hey, I placed higher than him. *I'm* your best player."

"Nah, you're not a player. You're some writer chick."

Adrian took advantage of her distraction with the phone and tickled her. She couldn't help the giggle that escaped her.

"Oh, my God, are you two in bed right now?" Connor sounded like he was being strangled. "Ew."

"Well, you shouldn't call a couple after ten on their honeymoon, idiot."

"You guys researching the next book already? Maybe the next one could be set in Atlantic City." He sounded hopeful. Right, that's where the next tournament was set. "You could come too. You could even tie it in to the last book. Have the same couple go there for a honeymoon, and stuff happens about their rushed marriage and his family."

Jenn stilled. "Oh, God, you read the book." Her heart pounded. Thousands of people had apparently read her book, but this was different. She'd purposely not given him a pre-release copy. Writing still occupied a tender spot in her heart, one that she wasn't sure could take the ribbing Connor liked to dish out when he thought he was being funny.

Adrian tensed a little under her and hugged her tightly. She looked into his eyes, and he gave her a small smile.

"I sent him a copy," he whispered.

"What?"

"Of course, I read the book. It was great. I'm so proud of you. Even if you do write porn."

"It's not porn!"

"Oh right, because they got married? It's porn. And let me tell you, if you and Adrian hadn't gotten married last week, he and I would be having a serious chat right now."

"No, you wouldn't. Everything in that book was completely from my imagination."

"Perv."

Jenn laughed, and Adrian relaxed and gave her another hug and a kiss on the forehead.

"I'll let you talk to him...later. We're busy."

"Ew again. Night sis. I'm proud of you. The book really is great."

"Night." She clicked off the phone and returned to kissing Adrian's shoulder. Maybe research wasn't such a bad idea.

"Everything cool?" He stroked her back, sending shivers of pleasure down her spine.

"Mmmm. You gave him a copy of my book."

"Yup."

She shook off the last of her tension. Adrian had struck again, looking out for her, helping her in a way that only he would know she needed help. God, she loved him. "He wants us to go to Atlantic City."

"Maybe. I might have used up all my luck when I asked you to marry me. I'm not sure I'd have any left for the game."

His hand slipped beneath the cover and cupped her bottom. He was already semi-hard beneath her belly. She scissored her legs open in response, straddling him, and moaned when he slid his fingers inside her.

She sucked in a breath when he found her clit. "Oh, I don't think so. I'm pretty sure you are about to get lucky right now."

He kissed her, taking her lips and tasting her like they

hadn't kissed a hundred times since that first time. Like they weren't married a week now and hadn't made love dozens of times in that week or even just an hour before. She would never get tired of the way he kissed. Not experiencing it in person, or writing about it.

Every goal she'd had that weekend in Las Vegas had been met and more. Everything in their lives had changed, except the way they felt about each other. That had been right since the first time he'd saved her. He still had tendencies to overprotect her, to want to take charge and take care of everything and everyone. She still had a nose for a bit of trouble. But they were good together—he could use a little trouble to take care of, and she really could use the research. Not everything that happened in Vegas stayed there.

In fact, it was coming out in her next book.

Thank you for reading! Please read on for a
sample of Between Moons by Lilly Cain
Now available for order here!

Between
Moons

LILLY CAIN

Prologue

"We'd like to congratulate Ms. Mathews on her recent closure of the largest deal this firm has seen in ten years. Raise your glasses and toast our sharpest nose for business, our shark in these shallow market waters, Ms. Helen Mathews!"

It was a perfect moment. The powerful owner of the company had his full attention on her. She looked fantastic, and the entire company had gathered to celebrate her promotion to partner, something she'd worked toward for the last few years with little time for anything else. The room was elegant—filled with white linen-draped tables topped with crystal and candles. The food was picture perfect, even if she couldn't bring herself to taste it. Her stomach twisted as she waited for his toast to continue and the announcement to be made.

Henry Winfield, President of Multoma, raised his glass of champagne and smiled at the gathered executives at the head table. In turn, they raised their glasses and smiled, although to most observers it probably looked more like the baring of teeth in a pack of wolves, with none willing to show a moment's weakness.

As Helen rose to accept her accolades, a disturbance at the back of the room drew the focus away from her and toward a small group of people. Two young men dressed in jeans and leather jackets pushed their way through the employees gathered in the hotel convention room, making way for an older woman. They rushed to reach the head table where Helen stood and the Board of Directors of Multoma Development International sat.

As they approached, the two men flanked the oddly dressed older woman. She seemed familiar, but Helen couldn't quite place her. The woman was perhaps in her seventies, and wore long, full skirts, a white blouse, and a ruby scarf wrapped around her waist as a belt. She was weighted down with rings on every finger, and wore her hair in a long, youthful hairstyle, even though it was fully gray. Her black eyes flashed at Helen, and her sneering smile was cold.

"Ms. Mathews." The old woman spoke, her clear voice belying any trace of age and certainly reaching all the corners of the room. "It is good to see that you're being recognized as the shark that you are—a predator that would eat its own young."

A collective gasp rippled through the room. Helen sucked in a breath, and lifted her chin in indignation. She felt her face flush, and felt the redness creep toward her neckline when she heard a few tittering laughs somewhere toward the back of the gathering. Annoyance had her gritting her teeth as she struggled to produce her usual professional smile. Already there were motions indicating that security had been called, so Helen remained standing, facing the odd group.

"Many thanks for the compliment." Helen controlled her voice to reflect only sarcasm, her intonation poisonous. "An insult so strong must indicate that I've moved up in the ranks of my critics' black list. However, now is not the time to trade respects. Perhaps you could reach me at the office for an appointment."

"I don't think so. We've had our meetings, and you've still ignored our claim to our rightful land. We don't ask for much. We rarely stay in one place, but still, we must have those few places where we can meet and be ourselves. The Rom will always be travelers, but you have taken away one of our last refuges."

As the old woman spoke, Helen suddenly realized who the person before her was. This was the same well-dressed, professional lawyer she'd been meeting with over a land dispute, a dispute involving the very deal she was being recognized for. Her people were the Rom—a branch of American Romanians that retained their wandering gypsy ways. They'd fought to keep the land—said it was their right to camp there annually as they had for generations, when in truth, the land belonged only to the government.

Sounds of approaching security personnel could be heard, and the woman glared hard at Helen and stroked a long, golden chain hanging about her neck. Her voice became more heavily accented, her phrasing more formal. "I curse you now, Helen Mathews. I curse you in the way of my people. I curse you three times as one who devours, as one who bares her fangs against those who would keep their own, and as the predator you truly are."

With a flick of her wrist the Rom woman reached into some hidden pocket within her skirts and pulled out a small bottle. In a fluid motion she flung it toward Helen. Helen stepped back but the tiny flask smashed against the table in front of her, splashing its contents out and upward, spattering Helen from head to toe.

By now, the old woman was shouting, racing to finish the words she now spoke in a foreign tongue before the guards dragged the uninvited accusers from the room. Helen stood frozen, caught in the spell of the Rom curse. She suppressed the urge to shiver, her blood running cold. She brushed her fingers over the flecks of liquid on her cheek. Everyone near her stared in hushed shock, even Mr. Winfield, a man she'd never seen off-pace. She looked down at her hand and realized she was covered in blood.

Chapter One

"Well, where the hell is she?" David Sherman's voice carried his annoyance clearly to the receptionist on the other end of the telephone. "I've been trying to reach Ms. Mathews all week. Does she *not* want to close this deal? There are at least two other companies I could go to with this. Understand?"

"I'm sorry, Mr. Sherman. Ms. Mathews will be returning to the office tomorrow. I'm sure she'll contact you right away."

"She'd better. We can't sit on this for much longer."

David hung up the phone and raised a hand to his aching head. What had he been thinking of, convincing himself that this woman was the only one for the job? That she was the only one that could make or break this deal? She'd been vague in her replies to his calls early last week, although she'd confirmed that the deal was one Multoma would be interested in. Then she'd simply disappeared, when they hadn't even yet met.

Her secretary couldn't even say where she was. Couldn't or wouldn't. David tensed as the thought occurred to him again that perhaps she had taken the idea he'd brought to the table and offered it to another firm. She was, after all, reputed to be absolutely ruthless. Since her apparent desertion after their last discussion, her absence was all he could think about.

David leaned back into his black leather chair, reclining as he considered the very real possibility of a double-cross. He had put together a tasty package of land just waiting for a big enough developer, and a plan to create a new retail and office center for Philadelphia. Would she steal that idea? He ran frustrated fingers though his hair.

She might. It was time to meet the woman in person. Time to get a better feel for her ethics. It was well known that she was strong, smart, and one of the best negotiators in the trade. She'd won concessions for developments from both the government and the public that no one had thought possible. It was because of her several unused and derelict sections of land, reclaimed from what used to be one of Detroit's largest dumps, were now being developed successfully into a huge science center and hospital. She'd been recognized by her company and made a senior partner, a feat practically unheard of for young a woman in this field.

David leaned forward and pressed the intercom button to summon his secretary. He looked around his spacious office. He was no small-time operator; he could take on this Helen Mathews. If she thought she could get away with stealing the biggest development he'd ever cultivated, she could think again. His corner office with a view in the largest office building in Philadelphia was proof of that.

Sally, a small but attractive young woman, entered the room quietly. For a moment David admired the cute blonde. She was just his type, blonde, curvy, and willing. And yet, there just wasn't any pull, any excitement, any challenge. Beyond that, he would simply never get involved with someone he worked with. He had more than enough proof that that path led to certain disaster.

"Can I help you, Mr. Sherman?" She paused in front of his desk, and leaned just a tad too far over, David noted. Although he certainly took a moment to admire the proffered view of her breasts, he was familiar with the pose. Women considered him handsome, but it was the power and money he controlled that seemed to be the deciding factor in their interest. Women loved power. It would be nice, if for once someone wanted him, not just the money and prestige that came with his lifestyle.

"I need travel arrangements to New York, Sally." David drew her attention back to work. Once, the kind of challenge she was silently offering would have aroused him, co-worker or not. He had to face it—he wasn't interested, and it wasn't because she worked for him. She was so much the same as the last three women he'd had affairs with, he couldn't bring himself to start the cycle again.

She straightened immediately and smoothed her skirt with ill-concealed irritation. He ignored it, what else could he do but pretend her silent offer had never happened?

"I want the next flight available. Book me first class and make reservations for dinner at that Japanese place, Ruby Foo's. They have private dining rooms. I'll be bringing a business prospect, so be sure we get it, no matter what we have to shell out. I'll stay at my apartment, so you know where to contact me."

David rattled off several more instructions and left a list

of reports he wanted generated and sent to him in New York. Within a few moments he was on his way out the door. It only occurred to him then that he hadn't soothed Sally's bruised ego. A quick cell call and an offer of the day off while he was gone was all it took. He could only hope that it would go as well with Helen Mathews.

Helen Mathews collapsed with exhaustion into her office chair. Any brief time away from her desk meant a huge pile of catch-up work, no matter how necessary the absence. Nearly a week off had left her an avalanche and her secretary and receptionist both looked at her as if she'd abandoned them. She simply could not explain to them why she'd left or where she'd gone.

Only their longtime loyalty kept them from asking too many questions. The two women had risen with her through the ranks of Multoma Developments and knew they owed her for the opportunities they had been given. Not one word had been said, at least not by them, not even when she knew they noticed a change in her appearance as well as habits.

Helen dug through the pile of papers left on her 'in' tray and sifted out the most important of the reports she'd requested before she left. How much longer could she keep this up? Surely, it wouldn't be long before someone else noted her absences. She pulled out the numbers on David Sherman's proposal. She'd only had time to skim it before she'd left last week. It was an excellent plan, one that combined land once considered unusable and therefore cheap, and an innovative architectural concept for engineering office space over what was basically a swamp.

She'd pulled all the information Multoma had on Sherman's past operations and on the man himself, and had taken it away with her. There were times when she could bring herself to read during her absence, although numbers were a near impossibility. There was a lot to review. He'd been a busy man over the last couple of years, and she discovered his ideas had proved quite interesting and profitable for Multoma before, although her team had never worked with him.

As for the man, she'd Googled him. She'd found more than she expected. According to the press, he'd never been married, had worked at the same firm until he became full partner, and was a serious contributor to various charities, including wildlife preservation. And yet, he was a hunter, well proven in his skill against wild game. He owned several apartments and condos across the country.

It was too bad she'd angered him by not contacting him last week. Her receptionist told her how irritated he'd been on the phone when he'd found out she'd left suddenly, but she could hardly have done otherwise. That thought brought her full circle.

She pulled off a pair of dark glasses to rub tired eyes. The shades were a permanent accessory now. She lay her head down on her desk, ready in that moment to weep. It was becoming too hard. Twice now she'd had to flee her office for an extended length of time. Twice she'd lied about it to coworkers and friends alike. One more time and she would likely be facing serious questions from her superiors about her ability to keep up her workload. Her father would be right, and she would fail. She was so tired.

Behind her eyelids she watched again the events of that horrible night replay like a tired movie. She couldn't escape the memory any more than she could escape the reality of her life since that moment. Helen's intercom chose that moment to buzz sharply, pulling her back to the present. A second after she jerked upright, the door opened.

"I'm sorry, Helen..." Sherry Davis, Helen's receptionist, spoke quickly from the hall, "but Mr. Sherman is here and insists on seeing you immediately." The middle-aged woman looked angrily over the top of her glasses at the man who pushed his way past her and through the door.

Helen stood to greet her uninvited guest. Her first impression of David Sherman tempted her to frown, although she held on to the expression as she'd trained herself to do. He was determined, and obviously irritated by her absence and her receptionist's protective attitude. Broad shouldered and thick through the chest, he towered over Sherry. Slightly too-long, light brown hair flipped arrogantly over his brow, and a long nose and smooth, strong jaw finished the frame of his face. Only his hazel eyes stood out as exceptionally beautiful; they brought his features together into a very pleasing form.

Before Helen could quite associate this handsome man with the phone calls she'd received a week ago, he was in her office and having his own good look at her. She flushed slightly as his eyes roved, but schooled her face into a pleasant mask. She was used to being inspected. It was all part of the business she had spent the last five years conquering.

She dressed the part of corporate executive-slash-warrior. Her tailored fuchsia suit fit her perfectly, and its bright color enhanced her pale skin and long black hair. She knew she looked tired, but as he stared at her longer and longer, she couldn't hold his gaze. What was he looking at? Did he see beyond her façade?

"Ms. Mathews, I'm David Sherman. I'm glad to finally

meet you." He extended his hand. His large, tanned fingers enclosed hers and she felt a tingle of attraction. She smiled at him, but sternly reminded herself of the many, many reasons she could not possibly become involved with anyone just now.

"Welcome, Mr. Sherman. I must apologize for not getting back to you sooner. I've been away on a business trip, as I'm sure my assistant informed you. I did, however, review the preliminary figures of your proposal."

Helen offered a chair with a wave of her hand as she lied though her teeth. She took her own seat, plunging into the details of the proposal. Without giving him an opportunity to comment on her absence, she lifted the page she thought indicated profit estimates from her desk, grateful that she'd at least had the time to pull the report from the pile of work on her desk and skim it before he arrived.

David reached for the paper, tugging it gently from her fingers. "Great percentages, don't you think? The lead indicators are well over the norm, and the market polls more than prove the need for these facilities in this location. It's hard to believe no one has acquired the land as yet." He smiled, looking pleased. His smile transformed his face from arrogant businessman to a ruggedly handsome man, and again she felt that zing of attraction.

"Yes, the numbers look interesting," Helen hedged. She had no idea what the percentages actually were, other than good.

"I'm glad to see you aren't letting a great deal slip away from Multoma. I was beginning to wonder if you were planning on passing it over to another firm." He looked at her calmly, apparently ignoring the fact that he was practically accusing her of stealing his pitch and perhaps even going behind the back of her own company. After a tense moment, his eyes shied to the left in a self-conscious movement.

"I see. Multoma does not operate that way, Mr. Sherman. Nor do I," she stated calmly. "My time is better spent as a negotiator than as a thief." She kept her face composed, but her stomach clenched. So much for attraction. This was only the first of the problems and accusations she'd likely face by having a forced monthly absence from the company. At least the man before her had the grace to eventually look embarrassed by his suggestion. There were many who wouldn't care that they were being offensive, not when it came to business.

"Well, you can hardly blame me for my suspicions. Not after you seemed to disappear. Let me take you out to dinner tonight to make up for it." His attitude changed perceptibly. He was apparently going to accept her at her word. "We can discuss the proposal then, and you can have today to catch up on all the paperwork that built up while you were away."

He stood, and handed back the paper. "This page, by the way, doesn't have any percentage numbers on it." He smirked, just a bit, and lifted an eyebrow. The scent of his cologne—woody and male—reached her and the attraction returned, sharper now. "Perhaps you could read the report before tonight. I'll send you my car." He didn't wait for her answer, pressing the advantage of having caught her unprepared for his visit.

"That would be fine," she said as he walked out the door. "Just fine." She slumped back into her chair and held her head in her hands. "Shit. Cocky asshole. Sexy, cocky asshole."

ACKNOWLEDGMENTS

Thank you to Cathryn Fox who worked with me on humor in novellas. :)

Note from Lilly:

I hope you really enjoyed this book! If you did, please leave a review on Goodreads or wherever else tickles your fancy.

For more stories from me, please check my website, www.lillycain.com or join my newsletter: http://www.lillycain.com/contact/

ABOUT THE AUTHOR

Lilly Cain is a wild woman with a deep, throaty laugh and plunging necklines. She is a great lover of all things sensual —perfume, chocolate, silk! She never has to worry about finding a date or keeping a man in line. She keeps her blond hair long and curly, wears beautiful clothes and loves loud music. Lilly lives her private life in the pages of her books.

All of the above is a bit of silliness. :) Lilly lives in Atlantic Canada, although she spent eight years in Bermuda, enjoying the heat and the pink sands. She returned to her homeland so she could see the changing of the seasons once again. When not writing she paints, swills coffee and vodka (but not together) and fights her writing pals for chocolate (true story).

When not living up to her pen name, Lilly is a single mom who loves reading and writing, dabbling in art and loving and caring for her two daughters. She loves romance and the freedom erotic fantasy provides her imagination. She loves the chilling moments in her novels as much as the steaming hot interludes. Her stories are an escape and a release, and she hopes that they can give you that power, too.

Connect with Lilly for info on her new releases,
access to exclusive offers and much more!
www.LillyCain.com
Lilly@Lillycain.com